Trouble on Tarragon Island

TROUBLE ON TARRAGON ISLAND

NIKKI TATE

WINLAW BRITISH COLUMBIA

Archives Canada Cataloguing in Publication

Tate, Nikki, 1962-
    Trouble on Tarragon / Nikki Tate.

(The Tarragon Island series ; bk. 3)
ISBN 1-55039-154-2

    I. Title. II. Series.

PS8589.A8735T76 2005   jC813'.54   C2005-904504-3

Sono Nis Press most gratefully acknowledges the support for our
publishing program provided by the Government of Canada through
the Book Publishing Industry Development Program (BPIDP), the
Canada Council for the Arts, and the British Columbia Arts Council.

Edited by Laura Peetoom, Dawn Loewen and Margaret Tessman
Cover painting by Ljuba Levstek
Cover and interior design by Jim Brennan

Published by   Distributed in the U.S. by
Sono Nis Press   Orca Book Publishers
Box 160   Box 468
Winlaw, BC V0G 2J0   Custer, WA 98240-0468
1-800-370-5228   1-800-210-5277

books@sononis.com
www.sononis.com

Printed and bound in Canada by Kromar
Printed on acid-free paper that is forest friendly (100% post-consumer
recycled paper) and has been processed chlorine free.

For Betty, Kate, and Doran,
real ladies of the forest

And for my mother, Helga,
lost but not forgotten

Acknowledgements

It's always a little unnerving to think of working with a new editor on an ongoing series: making the transition feels a bit like switching horses in the middle of a race. What a delight to find myself working with Laura Peetoom on this book. Laura, you are wise, funny, and demanding—the perfect combination of attributes for an editor!

Dawn Loewen, your eagle eyes always amaze me!

Several groups of women inspired Granny's transformation into an environmental activist: the Raging Grannies, the Women in the Woods, the women of Salt Spring Island who created the Save Salt Spring Calendar, and Briony Penn, who made headlines by riding her horse à la Lady Godiva to protest old-growth logging on Salt Spring Island.

Thank you to Corporal Grace Arnott of the Nelson RCMP detachment—that was a great tour of the lock-up. Who knew toilets came without seats!

From the very beginning, the title of this book caused everyone a lot of angst. Thank you to all the students at the Victoria, Chemainus, and Okanagan Young Authors Conferences for your fantastic suggestions. The title *Trouble on Tarragon Island* was submitted by so many of you we could hardly use anything else!

Diane Morriss, my publisher. What can I say? You are one of the very best in the business, and a good friend, too. Thank you for all that you do to allow Heather, Jessa, Dominique, and the rest of the gang to have new adventures. Without your continued support on so many levels I would have thrown in the towel long ago.

And, of course, many thanks to all the members of my wonderful family (is this starting to feel like an Oscar speech?) who bring me tea and keep me from straying too far off into la-la land.

If my animals could read, I would thank them, too, for keeping me sane in times of madness.

Thanks to everyone at Bolen Books who so graciously put up with the world's flakiest employee; the Smith-Nobbs clan who make me happy just because they are so alive in all their glorious, messy, loving chaos; Ljuba Levstek who captures the essence of story in her artwork; and the network of writers, reps, teachers, librarians, and booksellers across the country (and around the world) without whose tireless efforts there would be no publishing scene in Canada.

I know there are others who deserve to be recognized but given the state of my scattered files I will never be able to remember and thank you all. If you are one of those I have forgotten, be bold—send me an email and I'll get you next time!

1

No tears in the writer, no tears in the reader.

— Robert Frost

"Heeaaather . . ." Jerry Bastion's singsong voice taunts me, challenges me to turn around.

There's no way I'm going to stop walking. It's a safe bet that whatever the moron is going to yell next isn't going to be pleasant.

"Woo-hoo!" someone else hoots, and then gales of laughter stab at my back. A rude kissing noise right behind me makes the others howl even louder.

They must be laughing at my dumb skirt. Why did I wear it to school? It's short and kind of tight, well, tighter and shorter than I usually wear, but Granny took me over to Victoria to go clothes shopping and when I was standing in front of the full-length mirror at the Rage Boutique the skirt had looked cute. Granny said it made my legs look longer. In the store, I thought I looked thinner and that's why I agreed to buy the stupid thing.

I should know better than to listen to anything my

grandmother says these days.

"Yeeee-ow!"

The damned skirt makes me look like an idiot, like a girl who wants to be in the city, a girl who is acting like she wants to be a model except everyone knows she's too heavy and has the wrong shape of face—bulging cheeks, disappearing chin. Not that I want to be a model, I don't—I am going to be a writer. But face it, a skirt that's short and a bright colour (that's another problem, it's fuchsia with tiny white flowers in a swirl like the Milky Way circling over my backside), a skirt like that isn't going to make people say, "Hey, there goes a future Nobel Prize winner."

I've almost reached the end of the hall but the boys have not stopped their pursuit. One of them, probably Jerry the Jerk, lets out a long, wailing wolf howl. Despite the fact that I'm steeling myself, I jump and my pencil case slides off my pile of books.

Great. Now I have to stop, crouch down, and pick it up. What if the stupid skirt is folded up in the back or maybe—and this thought sends an even deeper blush swooshing directly to my brain—maybe I'm trailing a strip of toilet paper.

I grip my books in front of me, willing my hands to stay where they are even though they are dying to tug the bottom of the skirt down. Stiffly, I retrieve my pencil case and pretend that I don't hear Jerry smooching the air behind me. I'm almost at the sanctuary of the science lab.

And that's when it happens.

"Hey, Heeaather," Jerry drawls again, even louder. "Your grandma sure has saggy—"

"Shut up!" It's sickeningly clear now that all this unwanted attention has nothing to do with my skirt. A thousand details burn into my brain as I turn to face them. Jerry Bastion's mouth is stuck around the word he is about to say, his lips forming a hideous grimace, his forehead bisected by the plastic strap of his backwards cap. Does he not know how moronic he looks? How moronic they all look? Every single one of them is wearing a backwards baseball cap. Dan's arm is raised in the air just behind Jerry, about to slap his back. Ben's head is tilted up, his mouth yawns wide open with his tongue hanging out. And Simon has his hands cupped around two invisible melons suspended in front of him.

"Shut up!" I scream again, horrified at how loud I am, how everyone around us in the hallway slows down, stops to watch. With my second shriek, the boys unfreeze. Dan's hand slaps against Jerry's back and Jerry belts out, ". . . bazoongas!"

Simon and Ben double over, grabbing at each other's baggy shirts as they whoop and gasp. They are laughing so hard that tears wet Jerry's cheeks and he can't even speak.

Writer Girl's eyes blaze: the antics of the uneducated, unwashed mongrel boys deserve immediate punishment. Writer Girl throws her books at the leader's head. He drops to his knees, his hands clutching at the gash above his eye.

"Take it back," Writer Girl demands, waving the golden nib of her ten-thousand-dollar fountain pen under his nose.

Weeping with remorse, the mongrel boys apologize.

"We made it up—we'll never say stuff like that about your exalted grandmother again."

Of course, it doesn't go like that at all. I'm the one who stalks away, tears blistering my cheeks. The boys don't apologize—they howl. And why should they apologize? What they say about my grandmother is true. She does have generous bazoongas, and all of Tarragon Island has seen them.

2

Writing is the only profession where no one considers you ridiculous if you earn no money. – Jules Renard

"Heather? Is that you?"

A kind of paralysis seizes me and I stop halfway up the stairs. The last person I want to talk to is Granny. She pokes her head out the kitchen door and swings a dishtowel at me. "Trying to sneak in, are you?"

"No," I say, though that's exactly what I was doing. "I didn't think anyone was home."

"Where did you think I'd be?"

Oh, I don't know. Hugging a tree? Naked? I don't say that, though. I just shrug. "Where is everyone?"

"Your father's in his studio, Matt's next door with Alyssum, and your mom is at the Whittakers' place."

"Again?" The Whittakers have three horses and it seems as if each one of them has required attention during the past week. "What now?"

"I think the young one got caught up in some barbed wire. Your mom raced off to go and stitch her up."

I wince. I didn't inherit my mother's passion for animals, but even I know that horses and barbed wire don't mix.

"At this rate, the Whittakers will be putting you through college singlehandedly!"

Maybe I don't want to go to college. Maybe my novels will make me so much money I won't have to worry about getting some other kind of job. If Dad can make a living selling his paintings, then why can't I make mine writing books?

"Can you give me a hand moving the table?"

"The dining room table?"

"It's Thursday. The Ladies of the Forest are coming over."

I glance at my watch. 4:30. My writing group meets at the community centre tonight, but not until after dinner. I don't have any excuse not to help.

"I guess so."

"Don't sound so enthusiastic," Granny says and swats me on the backside with the dishtowel.

"Why do you have to move the table?"

"We're painting a banner. BIFI won't give up. They're scheduled to start cutting trees on Monday."

I drop my pack on the stairs and sigh. Granny is obsessed with BIFI, Burton International Forestry, Inc. The company is planning to log a bunch of trees on the south end of Tarragon Island and Granny is planning to stop them. Not by herself, of course. There are lots of people on Tarragon Island who want the Tarragon Woods to be protected and turned into a park. The Ladies of the Forest are a group of women, mostly older women, who meet every week at our house to plan how to get in the way of the loggers and save the trees. So far, they've drunk gallons of blackcurrant tea and consumed so many Nanaimo bars they must all be on the brink of developing diabetes. At least painting a banner sounds somewhat productive and definitely isn't the kind of thing you do naked.

Once the table has been moved, Granny asks, "When is your spring break?"

"Why?"

"Just curious. I thought we might spend a few days in Victoria. I haven't seen much of you lately."

Not so long ago, I would have jumped at a chance to get off this rock. Not so long ago, I thought my grandmother was relatively normal.

"I guess so."

Granny gives me a funny look before saying, "Let's go into the kitchen and I can mark the dates on the calendar."

The calendar. Deep in the pit of my stomach something folds over and turns inside out. I don't want to look at the calendar. It's disgusting. I can't believe Mom and Dad would let such a rude thing into the house, never mind hang it on the fridge where it's impossible to ignore. My brother, Matt, is only ten—he shouldn't have to look at that stuff every time he gets a drink of milk.

Granny is oblivious. She ignores the huge black-and-white photograph of Mrs. Haggerty fishing from a boulder in the middle of a stream. Mrs. Haggerty is older than Granny and in the photo she is stark naked. The way she holds her arms up with the fishing pole, you can't see anything, well, delicate. But even so . . . her toes are elderly toes, splayed over the slippery boulder just above the water and clinging like some great flabby bird's. The veins in her feet bulge and, most ludicrous of all, her toenails glisten with fresh nail polish. Because the photo is in black and white it's impossible to tell what colour she's wearing, but pink or red or whatever it is, the nail polish must have clashed with her knotty blue veins and purple-with-cold skin.

I know she must have been cold because the photos were taken back in early November. There was a huge rush to get the calendars out before Christmas. I must have been the only person on the island who was disappointed when, against all odds, they made it with days to spare. Enough days, in fact, for the crazy old women to sell more than two thousand copies, to be hung on family fridges across the land. Yuck.

Granny flips Mrs. Haggerty out of the way and runs her finger along the numbered boxes.

"The last day of school is the eleventh of March," I say, blushing. "We go back on the twenty-first." Slowly, neatly, Granny draws a red line across the days and writes in: *Heather Off. Spring Break.*

"So, would you rather go away at the beginning or the end of your break?"

I'd rather go away now so I don't have to stare at the Ladies of the Forest having a picnic in the Tarragon Woods. The month of March shows four old women sitting on a checkered tablecloth spread beneath the trees. Two of them hold teacups and saucers, another holds a china teapot, and another very old, very wrinkled woman balances a plate of little sandwiches with one hand. The other hand is on her hip and she's laughing as if someone has just told her a very funny joke. I don't find any of it amusing because the only things the women are wearing are huge, floppy, flowery old-lady hats. Big as these hats are, they don't cover much. I can see every wrinkle, sag, bag, and liver spot on parts of ancient bodies that should never be exposed to the air.

I turn away and head for the cookie jar even though I'm not the least bit hungry. That photograph on the fridge is enough to turn anyone's stomach. It's only the middle of January. We have eleven more horrible naked-old-lady pictures to suffer through between now and the end of the year.

"Well?"

I can't even remember what Granny wants to know.

"Beginning or end of the break?"

I couldn't care less. "Middle, I guess."

Granny raises her pen as if to write and then hesitates. "Now that I think about it, either weekend would be better—the loggers don't work then. If we're still protesting."

"Fine. Whatever. Do whatever you want."

"Heather—"

"The last weekend," I say. "So I have something to look forward to." The last part is a lie, but I say it to get Granny off my case. Really, I suggest the last weekend so I can delay for as long as possible any time I have to spend with my grandmother. She's losing her mind and I don't want anything to do with it.

3

To avoid criticism, do nothing, say nothing, be nothing.
— Elbert Hubbard

I arrive at the Tarragon Island Community Centre just after seven. I'm not the only one running on island time. Eric sprints up the front stairs right behind me and says "Boo!" in my ear.

"Hi, turkey."

Eric grins, pushes past me, and opens the front door with a flourish.

"After you, madam."

The community centre is actually a big, old-fashioned house that has been converted into a preschool, meeting rooms, a small community hall, and a couple of offices. We meet in a room that looks more like a living room than anything else. The fireplace is bricked up, but the first person to arrive always turns on a space heater to take the chill off the air. The room is already toasty warm and I peel off my scarf and sweater as we walk in.

The usual kids are sitting in their usual places: Wynd Bell on her cloak on the floor and Gillian Wong on the couch with her fat binder open across her knees and her feet in their embroidered red slippers propped up on the coffee table. I like Gillian—she's sort of the embodiment of innocence, if I'm going to be poetic about it. Eric slides into his usual place on the floor under the coffee table and begins rooting around in his bookbag. It's only then that I really notice who else is here.

The boy is what I'd call lanky, if I were putting him in a book. He's maybe thirteen or fourteen and his limbs make up 90 percent of his body mass. His fingers are long, too, stretched across the back of his notebook as he scribbles. His spindly digits remind me of one of those tree frogs from the jungles of South America. Some of those frogs have long toes with bulbous, sticky ends so they can cling to slick banana leaves or mirrors or whatever South American tree frogs cling to. Frog Boy is completely absorbed in what he's doing, which isn't writing, but drawing little cartoon people with thought bubbles above their heads. The back of his notebook is covered with scratchy drawings, squiggles, patterns, and words like *Bif!* and *Whammo!*

He doesn't even seem to notice Willow, who sits on the loveseat beside him. I'm used to Willow now, but when I first came to Tarragon Island and joined TWYG (the Tarragon Writing Youth Group), she scared me to death. As usual, she looks as if she has one foot in the grave because her face is so white. The effect of the powder Willow wears is enhanced by the black outlines around her eyes and her glistening scarlet lipstick, so vivid it looks as though she's just dipped her mouth in a puddle of blood. Black hair, glossy like a raven's feathers in the sun, tops off the whole effect.

The other new kid is sitting on the couch beside Gillian. She also has her feet stretched out in front of her, but her hiking boots rest on top of a solid-looking leather bag instead of the table. Or maybe it would be more accurate to call it a satchel. Briefcase. I haven't ever seen a bag quite like it. It reminds me a bit of the kind of suitcase that travelling salesmen have, full of samples and invoices and business cards. She wears wire-rimmed glasses and has a kerchief over her head, which strangely enough doesn't make her look like some time-travelling flower child out of the 1960s, but instead makes her look perky. Cute. Maybe it's because the kerchief is a wild pink and orange print and she's tied it behind her head instead of under her chin. Or maybe it's the way she's watching everyone and everything with her wide, dark eyes, as though she's drinking in the scene and will write everything she sees in her notebook later.

She notices me noticing her and she smiles and says, "Hi! I'm Karin!" Her voice is warm and intelligent and it reminds me of something Matt told me. He said that people form their first impressions of you in just three seconds and that first impressions are really hard to change. In the three seconds I've known Karin, I form the impression that she is someone I would like and so I smile back at her and hope she feels welcome.

"Welcome!" Eric says from the floor. Karin rewards him with a really big grin and a friendly laugh.

"Thanks! I'm so glad you guys have room in the group!"

She moves over, makes a space for Eric beside her, pats the couch cushion, and, miracle of miracles, Eric pulls himself out from under the table and sits beside her!

I want to kick him, or myself. Why didn't I welcome Karin out loud? Then I could have sat beside her. As it is, the only place left to sit is on the fat armchair over by the window. I hate sitting there because I don't feel like part of the group. I guess I could move the chair, but it weighs about 87,000 kilos and I don't want anyone to think I'm that needy.

"Eric," Eric says and stretches out his hand. "Pleased to meet you." The greeting is unbearably hokey, but both Eric and Karin are still grinning.

"The pleasure is all mine," Karin says, and they both crack up.

"This should be good," Wynd says. "Two comedians."

"That's Wynd," Eric says, pulling a face. "Gillian, Willow, Heather, and—" He stops and looks expectantly at Frog Boy on the loveseat.

"Custer."

"Custer?"

"Yeah. Like the Last Stand."

Poor kid. What a name. Unlike Karin, who looks totally at home as she opens her narrow notebook, the kind where you flip the pages up and over the spiral wire coil, Custer drops his head and concentrates on whatever it is he's drawing now. He's lifted his notebook up on his knee so I can't see anything any more.

"Welcome, Custer," Willow says. Though the words

she says are perfectly normal, something in the way she says them makes Wynd snort.

"Excuse me for living," Willow says, and waves her hand as if she's brushing away a fly. "So, Custer. Tell us what you like to write. I'm into death and suffering myself."

"And poetry and fiction nobody understands," Eric adds.

"Shut up." Turning back to Custer, Willow continues. "Did you bring something to read?"

Custer turns bright red. "I guess. Well . . . I don't really . . ."

His voice trails off and he starts scribbling again. I want to rip the pen out of his hand and throw it out the window.

"Lay off, Willow," Eric says. "We have a policy that new people don't have to read the first couple of times they come if they don't feel comfortable. But after that, if you want to keep coming, you have to bring work to share."

Custer's blush gets even deeper. I wonder if it's possible to burst something if so much blood flows to your head. Or maybe your foot would get gangrene because all the blood from the extremities has flooded to your cheeks. Do eyeballs fill up with blood when a person blushes? Could eyeballs ever burst from extreme embarrassment? All these idiotic thoughts pop in and out of my head as I watch poor Custer struggle to come up with something to say.

"It's not that I don't feel . . . that I . . . I just . . ."

The more he stammers, the harder we listen. There

isn't another sound in the room except for Custer fumbling around for words.

"Do you mean that I have to read out loud if I want to keep coming?"

I wonder if Custer is dyslexic or something. My brother Matt would rather pull out his fingernails one by one than read aloud. I'm about to say something to defend Custer when Eric says, "I guess someone else could read your selection aloud for you."

Custer shakes his head. "That's not it. I just don't know how to read my stuff aloud." He flips his notebook open and shows it to Eric and Karin.

"Oh," Eric says.

"Wow!" Karin says, handing back the book.

I can't stand it. I feel as if I'm not even attending the same meeting. I get out of my chair, march around behind the loveseat, and bend over so I can see.

"What? That's not writing!" I blurt out. Custer hasn't brought a story or a poem. His work is some kind of comic strip.

"Let me see," Wynd says, and takes the notebook. Gillian and Willow bend their heads over Custer's work and study it. Poor Custer looks like he's been pricked with a huge needle. He slumps back into the loveseat with his long fingers interlocked, clamped together as if he's trying to stop them from fluttering away.

"Sure it's writing," Willow says. "What do you call this?" She points at words in a box above a rough sketch of a fat cat sitting on a windowsill. *"Martin couldn't bear the thought of another day without tuna."*

I roll my eyes and plunk myself back into the armchair. What next? Will we be letting in the people who write the dumb jokes they stick inside bubble-gum wrappers?

"That's not my best work," Custer says. "I write about all kinds of things. War. Depression. Looting. Rock bands."

"See. Worthy subjects," Willow says.

Gillian still hasn't said anything. "You know," she says finally. "I'm not really sure . . ."

Wow. That's pretty negative, for Gillian. She's the youngest of the group and usually pretty quiet. If I had to criticize her critiquing technique it would be to say that she is too kind. For the same reason, I love it when she makes a comment about my work. It's like an antidote or salve to the toxic comments that the others sometimes come up with.

"What about you?" Eric asks. "What do you think, Karin?"

I shift in my chair. Why is he asking her? She hasn't even been a member of the group for five minutes. She shouldn't have a vote! She doesn't know what kind of a group we are. Maybe she isn't even a serious writer herself!

"I loved *Persepolis*," she says. "Have you read it?"

Custer straightens right up and his hands fly to his hair. "You've read *Persepolis*? That's a great book! I wish I could write something like that!"

"What's *Persopholis*?" I ask. "Some kind of Greek tragedy?"

Karin and Custer look at me pityingly. "*Per-SEP-olis,*"

they say together. "It's a graphic novel," Karin adds.

"Graphic novel? Like porn?" Gillian asks, her eyes about ready to pop out of her skull.

"What's *Per-SEP-olis* about?" I ask, pretty sure no kid who looks like a frog would dare show up at a writing group with lewd material.

"As a Western woman, you really should read it," Karin says. "It's about this girl who grows up in Iran and is oppressed and can't go out without a male relative to chaperone her. It's a really, really interesting statement about freedom."

"Oppression. Freedom. Nothing wrong with subjects like that," Willow says.

"That's my point, Willow—you just can't say anything really meaningful in a comic book." I want to make her understand. What Karin says next doesn't help my case.

"But you can in a graphic novel. *Persepolis* is a real book that uses comic strips to tell a real story. An important story."

I hear the words they are saying, but I still find it hard to believe that anyone could take thought balloons seriously.

Eric says, "I think maybe we have to give Custer a chance. Why don't we see what his work is like and make a decision after, I don't know, one month? Three more meetings. Then we'll take a vote. Unless someone else can think of a better way."

Nobody says anything, though Custer doesn't look too impressed.

"Okay. Custer, you can stay—for now. Maybe you can

bring photocopies of whatever it is you're working on so we can read along and critique both the artwork and the writing?"

Karin nods. "That's a good idea."

I don't find her voice so friendly anymore. Instead, her cheery cooperativeness grates on my nerves. I wish I hadn't come tonight. I should have stayed home and . . . and . . . and what? Work on my novel? If I didn't have the writing group to come to, some weeks I don't think I'd write a single word. As it is, the stuff I bring isn't always very good, but at least I've produced something. And not comic strips, either.

"What about you, Karin? What do you write?" Eric asks.

Karin smiles again. "I don't know if I should tell you."

Wynd and Willow exchange glances. "I can't imagine," Wynd says.

"I'm sure it will be fine. Do you also write comics?" Eric asks.

Karin shakes her head. "Not exactly—although my storyboards sometimes look a bit like comic strips."

"Storyboard? What's that?" Gillian asks. "Isn't that what picture book illustrators use?"

"Maybe they do, I don't know. It's the plan I make when I'm getting ready to make a new film."

"Film?!" The word pops out of my mouth before I can stop it. I know how disgusted I sound but I can't even think of a way to apologize. Film? Where's the writing in pointing a camera at someone?

"You're a filmmaker?" Eric sounds way too impressed.

I just know he's going to side with her.

"What kind of films?" Willow asks. "Do you write the scripts?"

Grudgingly, I have to admit that creating a script would be a kind of writing.

"Sometimes. Sometimes I collaborate. It depends on what kind of thing I'm creating. If it's like a feature film, then, yeah—I need a script. And even for a documentary I need a kind of a script—a plan for shooting."

"That's not writing," I say, "having a plan. I have a lot of plans in my head for novels I might write one day. But until it's down on paper it hardly counts."

"I beg to differ," Karin says, apparently oblivious to the fact she talks like someone in an old movie. Though she should probably be mad, she isn't. She just smiles and launches into this long explanation about how much planning she does before even picking up her video camera. "Even a documentary has to tell a story. If some part of the story is missing, or badly done, people won't watch— or they'll start watching and get bored—or they'll get to the end and feel dissatisfied, just like with a novel." Karin looks right at me when she says that.

"Are you working on a movie right now?" Gillian asks, her dark eyes wide open, her pen poised over a blank sheet of paper as if she's about to take notes.

Karin nods. "Yeah. I love this island. We haven't lived here for very long but there are tons of really good stories. I like making documentaries because I think the stuff real people do is way more interesting than anything you could ever make up."

That's true. The challenge of writing is to shape the facts into good stories. And it doesn't really matter what kind of writing it is. Even novels set in exotic places about people doing exciting things have to seem believable—and making characters believable has a lot to do with paying attention to all the wacky things people get up to.

Still, I'm not convinced. So what if we have the same ideas about what we do? This is a writing group, for *writers*. Karin should go and find herself a filmmaking group.

"So, what's your movie—"

"Documentary."

"—documentary about?" Eric asks.

"I'm so excited about this one," Karin says. "Tons of drama, really amazing people being brave and noble."

"On this rock?" I say. "You've got to be kidding!"

"Haven't you heard about the war in the woods?"

A horrible, wobbly feeling seeps into my legs and my mouth goes dry. "What woods?" Though I know perfectly well what she's going to say.

"You know—the Tarragon Woods. There's this bunch of crazy old ladies who are protesting against the logging companies. You wouldn't believe some of the things they do to get their point across."

"Oh, them," I say, and glare an "I'll kill you, Eric Maloney" eyeball blast right at him.

Eric answers my silent message with a quick, knowing glance and a wink. He knows about Granny and he also knows that I absolutely do not wish to discuss the bizarre stuff she does in her spare time. If he says anything, I will never, ever come back to TWYG. Ever.

"That's a fascinating subject," Eric says, though it sounds as if he's trying really hard not to laugh. "I think we should have the same rules for you as for Custer. You can bring stuff—storyboards or scripts or videos or whatever—for the next month and then we'll take a vote."

I fix my gaze on Custer and give him a little encouraging smile. It wouldn't be cool to vote both of them out—I'd just seem embittered, or jealous or something. But if one of these two fake writers has to go, I'd rather it was Karin. I cannot imagine any fate more dreadful than having to sit in the same room with these kids and watch my grandmother do who-knows-what on film. My only hope is that Karin doesn't get to film Granny between now and the time her probation period is up.

Apparently, I'm not the only one who is perturbed about the subject of Karin's film. Gillian sits forward in her chair and says, "Those people are crazy. They don't care about the families who work in the forest industry or what they'll do if they aren't allowed to cut trees. Don't they know that trees grow back?"

Gillian isn't usually so vocal. She takes another deep breath and continues. "I don't think you should waste your time filming freaks who have no respect for working people. They're all rich know-it-alls from the mainland with nothing better to do, people who have never had to work and don't know what it's like to—"

She stops as suddenly as she started, her bottom lip quivering.

"Your dad works for BIFI, doesn't he?" Wynd says.

Gillian nods and wipes her eyes with the back of her hand.

"Sorry," Karin says. "I didn't know."

"So you'll find another subject?"

"I don't think so. But you could make a film about the other side of the story. That would be interesting—we could have a screening and show both films together and then have a discussion afterwards . . ." Karin's voice trails off. Gillian's bottom lip is wiggling again.

"I don't make films. I'm a writer," Gillian says.

It's all I can do not to jump up, applauding. I didn't think Gillian had it in her to take on someone like Karin. That's at least two votes against Karin, the imposter.

"Might I suggest we commence with the work of the evening?" Eric says, and everyone nods and shuffles papers with an unusual degree of enthusiasm.

4

Monotonously the lorries sway, monotonously come the calls, monotonously falls the rain. It falls on our heads and on the heads of the dead up the line, on the body of the little recruit with the wound that is so much too big for his hip; it falls on Kemmerich's grave; it falls in our hearts.

— Erich Maria Remarque, "All Quiet on the Western Front"

It's only after I hop in and slam the car door that I look at the driver.

"Mom?"

Usually Dad picks me up after meetings in town—Mom likes to put her feet up after a day in the vet clinic. It's a touchy subject. Once I made the mistake of asking Dad if he minded the fact that his wife was the one with the real job. "What are you doing here?"

"Hi, Heather. How was the group?"

"Sorry. Hi. What are you doing here?"

"Your father was busy, so here I am. Acceptable? Now, how was your writing group?"

I'm not sure exactly how a simple exchange of greetings deteriorated into something that feels suspiciously like an argument. "Fine."

"That's it? Fine?"

"Fine."

"Doesn't sound fine to me. What happened? They didn't like your writing?"

My determined silence has no effect.

"Did someone new join the group?"

Still no answer.

"Heather. Why can't you answer a simple question? Why do you have to make things so difficult?"

Me? Why does she have to ask so many questions? I wish Mom could just pout to herself and drop the whole subject, but I can tell she isn't going to let this go. Her dogged persistence, as she likes to remind us from time to time, is what got her through vet college even when she had to work two jobs so she could afford to buy the textbooks she needed and not get evicted.

"What makes you think there were new members?"

"More than one?"

"Two. Both strange."

"There was a car I didn't recognize out in the parking lot. I seem to remember you thought they were all strange when you started. You get along fine with the other kids now, don't you?"

Until tonight's meeting, I would have grudgingly agreed that even though there is a certain quirkiness to each of the members of our group, they are all basically pretty cool people. Now, though, it feels like people are warming up to engage in a battle to the death. Given the rising tension in the car, I figure silence is the safest option and rest my head against the window with an "I'm tired" that I hope sounds weary enough to be convincing. After maybe a minute of listening to my heavy breathing and the squeaky *flippa-welch* of the windshield wipers, Mom switches on the radio and we survive the trip home without more strife.

When Mom and I finally arrive home and walk up to the house, the lights are blazing, though until we open the door we don't see anyone inside. It turns out that's because everyone is grovelling around on the floor.

"What are you doing down there?"

"What does it look like—baking cookies."

"Smart ass." I wish Matt and Dad *were* baking cookies. They are actually down on the floor on their hands and knees wedged between two Ladies of the Forest and Granny. Yet another long fabric banner cloaks the kitchen floor and stretches all the way over to where our dining room table should be.

Each person is painting a bright red letter. When Matt sits back on his heels to see how his "O" is coming along, I read, "STOP THE SLAUGHTER!" Red dribbles streak the bottom half of the banner and a crudely painted axe jabs into the letter "S" of SLAUGHTER.

"That's catchy. I didn't think you could slaughter trees. As far as I know, they don't bleed, either." Despite a warning look from Dad, I don't stop. "You're a cute little lady of the forest, Matt."

Matt flicks his paintbrush at me. "Hey! Act your age!"

Instead of getting mad at Matt, Dad says, "That's enough, Heather. If you're not interested in the project, you have a room to go to."

"Or a chicken coop," Matt adds, getting a last dig in about my renovated writing cottage.

Mom is right behind me, so when I turn to go back outside I crash straight into her. I fully expect she's going to get mad, too, but she doesn't. Instead, she rolls her eyes and turns around and follows me out.

"Don't get so annoyed, Heather. When your grandmother loses interest she'll find herself another project."

"Knitting would be good," I say, and to my surprise, Mom laughs.

"Scarves, you mean?" Mom punches me in the shoulder. "Gotcha," she says. Granny's picture in the infamous calendar shows her knitting an impossibly long scarf, which unfortunately is still not long enough to cover everything that should be covered.

"Gotcha back." I punch her shoulder, just like we used to do when I was little. Then I remember I'm still mad at her for being nosy and thinking she knows everything about my life so I stalk across the driveway as well as I can in the dark and feel my way into Dove Cottage. It doesn't seem worth the effort to slam the door, so I push it closed softly and grope for the lamp on the desk.

Once I can see, I pull my journal from its hiding place behind a loose board in the wall above the window, pull my long sleeves over my hands to keep them warm, and settle down at the desk to write.

Thursday January 20th
I know I am supposed to write in my journal about things

that are going on in my life, but everything that is going on makes me mad so I'm going to write about something else.

Of course, it's easy to write that, but what the heck am I actually supposed to write about if I'm not going to mention anything that's going on? I read in a book somewhere that if you are a writer and you really get stuck, you should just write "I have nothing to write. I have nothing to write." You do that over and over again and eventually your pen gets bored and other words start flowing.

I can vouch for the fact that this system does not work for everyone. I once filled up three pages of a journal with *I have nothing to write* until my hand started to ache and I couldn't be bothered any more. The thought of three more pages of *nothing to write* is beyond depressing. Instead I decide to write to Maggie.

Tarragon Island, BC,
Canada, North America, World, Universe
Thursday January 20th
Dear Maggie

The pen stops on its own, a strange phenomenon that has been happening more and more often when it comes to writing to my old best friend. I guess that's not totally accurate—Maggie is not old and maybe she's not my best friend. And it's not just writing to her that's hard these days, it's writing anything at all, especially stuff that's personal. The thing is, when I used to live in Toronto, Maggie and I talked about everything, so writing a letter about how great the weather is on the West Coast would almost seem rude. Besides, I don't think the weather here is all that it's cracked up to be. So I'm stuck: I can't write about trivial matters and I sure don't want to tell her what's really going on.

Which is too bad because I could write pages and pages about the rain. When Mom looks out the window and sees the trees at the end of the driveway cloaked with mist and everything soaking wet and the thick curtain of water overflowing the eavestroughs, she doesn't say, "Damn, more rain!" She says, "At least you don't have to shovel it." She may have a point there—we have a very long driveway—but I still think a bit of shovelling is worth the crisp bite of a frosty morning and the soft, wet melt of snowflakes on my cheeks and eyelashes. Here, if you tip your head back and stick out your tongue, you're likely to drown.

Like right now it's bucketing down—it sounds as if a thousand baby goats are dancing on the roof of Dove Cottage. That may sound like a crazy metaphor, or simile, or whatever it is, but around here, stranger comparisons could be made.

Our neighbours, the Cranwells, have goats and they live in an underground house. The Cranwells, I mean, not the goats. The goats often graze up on the roof, which is really the ground. The grass is pretty thick up there, so maybe the noise is more like muffled thuds than spattering marbles.

Not that any of this really matters because I have no intention of boring Mags to death with details of the weather on Tarragon Island.

I add "Dove Cottage" at the top of the sheet of paper and stop again. As I think, I run my thumbs up and down the ragged edges of the handmade paper. I bought exactly three sheets from Tonya Windwoman, the paper lady at the Saturday market. It's gorgeous stuff—thick and cream-coloured with rose petals and bits of fern embedded right into the paper. It's so special, I don't want to mess it up by writing something dumb, boring, or forgettable.

You'll never guess what Granny has been doing.

Now what? How can I possibly admit that my grandmother ripped her clothes off with a bunch of her friends to save some dumb trees? There are lots of trees on this island. I don't see what all the fuss is about.

Granny has become an environmental activist.

I unfold the newspaper clipping from the *Tarragon Times* and study it again. Even if I cut off the photo of some of the Ladies of the Forest, the article still isn't safe to send to Maggie. " *'There is nothing more natural than the human body,' says Mrs. Watkins, one of a dozen women, all senior citizens, who created the* Bare Facts *calendar to raise funds for their environmental protests. 'And there's nothing more unnatural than the way the foreign-owned forestry companies come here and clear-cut our forests.'* "

The article goes on and on, quoting the different

women and explaining why they are taking turns blocking the road leading to the Tarragon Woods. There's no interview with anyone from the logging company, though, and that doesn't seem quite fair to me. I guess maybe Mr. Turnbull at the paper probably agrees with the Naked Ladies Brigade—or maybe he just thinks pictures of them are more interesting than some old, fat guy with a hard hat and chainsaw.

I suck on the end of my pen. If only I could psychically beam my thoughts all the way to Ontario and Maggie could pick up everything all at once so I didn't have to explain. Then Mags could beam back one of her stupid smiles and a hug and I wouldn't care so much about Granny's sudden transformation into some kind of geriatric superhero.

I think we should try a mental telepathy experiment. What if we choose a date and a time and then go somewhere quiet and focus on a specific object, like think about it really hard. Then, the other person writes down anything that pops into her head.

I stop writing because right away I can see a problem. If we are both concentrating on objects, how can we also be writing down what we think the other person is thinking about? Our thoughts could get all tangled up. I almost laugh out loud because I get this crazy picture of Mags staring at her cat and me staring at a dictionary and then seeing a tail with words hanging from it and Maggie seeing a book with little kittens squished flat between the pages. I saw a book like that at Wise Owl Books down in Rosehip except the drawings are of dead fairies that have been caught between the pages. It's kind of disgusting, but I kept turning the pages to see the expressions on the dead fairies' faces: shock, surprise, contentment, terror.

I stare at the unfinished letter. The paper is too good to throw out and I'm trying to be really careful and use a good pen so my handwriting is unusually neat.

Change of plans. We can set up a schedule.
Thursday, January 27, 6:30 p.m.: You send, I receive.
Thursday, January 27, 7:00 p.m.: I send, you receive.

Then I realize the date won't work because I'll be rushing off to my writing group. And the time won't work for Mags either because it's three hours later in Ontario.

Another change of plans—ignore what I just wrote up there.
Sunday, January 30, 11 a.m. my time (2 p.m. yours): You send, I receive.
Sunday, January 30, 11:30 a.m. my time (2:30 p.m. yours): I send, you receive.
Call or email me if the date and times are okay.

The page is nearly full and it looks a mess. I should have just sent an email, except I have to use the computer in the office when Mom closes up the clinic for the day all the rest of us are competing to get on the Internet.

We've got a schedule to try to stop the arguments but

nobody ever gets enough time. Matt always tries to get a few more minutes; he figures he deserves it since he schools at home and is a slow reader. But if Dad says he's doing research, Matt and I get kicked off the computer anyway. The last time I tried to write to Mags, Dad said that no real writer can craft a decent letter, a letter worth keeping, using email. I don't know if I agree with the part about not writing well on the computer—I'm pretty good at composing stuff and making changes right on the screen—but he is right about creating something worth keeping.

Gorgeous paper. A good pen. The fact my hands have touched the same page and folded it into an envelope that Mags will later open and smooth flat as she reads— that's special. Better than email. I like to add things to letters, too. Once I put in a cherry-flavoured candy worm and Mags said it got squished all over the page and left a stain but she loved it anyway.

So, all in all, even though the letter is a bit of a mess, I decide to send it. Before I sign my name at the bottom, I scratch out the last part and write,

Just phone or email if the times won't work.

Then I crease the paper in thirds, slip the message into a matching envelope, and take it into the vet clinic. Milly, Mom's receptionist, will find it in her "Mail Out" basket tomorrow morning and then the message will be on its way.

5

The writer's only responsibility is to his art. He will be completely ruthless if he is a good one ... If a writer has to rob his mother, he will not hesitate; the Ode on a Grecian Urn is worth any number of old ladies.

— William Faulkner

I have two words to say to Mr. Faulkner: Jane Austen.

— Laura Peetoom

On Saturday when I get up, Mom is already in the clinic and Dad and Matt are making blueberry pancakes.

"Smells good," I say, pouring a little syrup out of the squeeze bottle onto my fingertip.

"Heather!"

Dad makes me jump and I dribble on the floor.

"I wouldn't have spilled any if you hadn't yelled at me!" I lick my finger and then mop up the sticky spill with a wet paper towel.

"Are you busy this morning?"

Being half asleep and in a good mood because of the

pancakes, my guard isn't up, so I shake my head.

"That's good."

"Why?" But it's too late to back out now. Dad has been making plans.

"Matt and I are going to take some food up to the blockade. I think you should come."

"What? Why can't you two just go? You're all excited about what they're doing."

"Heather. Your grandmother is standing up for what she believes in. It's hard enough to be on the front lines without her having to worry about what her own family will say."

"Hard? They just sit around in the woods and have tea! They don't even bother to get dressed!"

Matt blushes and pulls a loaf pan out of the oven. Banana bread. One of my absolute, all-time favourites, especially the way Matt makes it, with lots of walnuts.

"How long will the pie take, Matt?" Dad asks.

Matt checks the timer on the stove and adjusts the temperature dial. "About twenty minutes."

"Be ready to go in half an hour," Dad tells me.

I know there's no room to argue. Dad doesn't often tell us what to do—he's more the kind of guy who likes to talk things through and then hopes his gentle persuasion will make you see things his way. I suppose he knows that no amount of gentle persuasion would get me into the truck to drive out to the blockade with them and has decided to use the direct approach.

"Fine. I'm going to eat in my room. Call me when I have to go."

Watching me balance my plate, cutlery, and a big glass of milk, Dad looks as if he wants to say something else, but thinks better of it and turns back to Matt instead. "Are you going to leave that in the loaf pan? Or cool it on the rack?"

I don't stick around long enough to hear what Matt says. It's ridiculous that we are encouraging the Ladies of the Forest to behave the way they do by feeding them. If nobody brought any food, they wouldn't last long out there in the woods. I bet none of them have a clue about what wild foods they could eat or how to snare a rabbit. Not that I like the idea of all those old people running around with sharpened sticks like some wrinkled version of the kids in *Lord of the Flies*. But still, if nobody paid much attention to what they were doing, I bet they'd come home and behave themselves.

The rain has not let up for days. For a little while this morning the grey clouds looked a little higher, lighter, but instead of growing brighter, the sky darkened again and the rain beat on the roof over my bedroom as if it wanted to come inside and swamp me. When we climb into the truck, the puddles are thick with mud and dimpled with raindrops. Mia, our Yorkshire terrier, was outside just long enough to sprint to the side of the driveway for a quick piddle before hopping in the truck, but the whole cab stinks of wet dog. It's amazing, really, considering how small she is. Her panting steams up all the windows. The defroster on the old truck doesn't work too well, so I lean forward to wipe away the fog with the back of my hand.

"Don't. You'll make it smeary."

As if that matters. Better we can see the big world out there through a smeary windshield than not at all.

"Here. Use this."

"Oh, Dad."

Dad has always said that the soft, fine cotton of old underwear makes the best paint rags. But wiping the window with a pair of Mom's old undies? That's a bit much.

"They're clean," he says.

"Disgusting," Matt says, firmly holding onto the corners of the baking pan that's on his lap, topped by a pie plate.

Dad reaches over and wipes the windshield himself, balls up the offending cloth, and tosses it over his shoulder into the back with Mia. "Stop breathing back there," he says. "At least until we arrive."

I don't know why it is that I'm much more likely to get carsick when it's raining. Maybe it's because the horizon disappears when the sky, the water, the road, the ground, and the trees all fuse into a grey sheet of miserable non-colour. Maybe it's psychological. Maybe I know that the most sensible place to be in weather like this is somewhere warm, dry, and stationary.

When I complain to Dad about how my stomach feels after a couple of minutes on the twisty logging road, he doesn't say anything, just sighs through his nostrils and turns the windshield wipers up higher. Matt moves his hands so they protect his precious baking.

But I'm in no danger of losing the contents of my stomach. Sometimes I think I would feel better if I did. Instead, I can practically feel my skin shifting from its normal pinky beige tone to green. Putrid pea green is about how I feel as we approach the encampment on the road.

We don't actually see the women at first because we have to park at the very edge of the road behind several large trucks. They look like graders and dump trucks and every one of them is emblazoned with the black emblem of Burton International Forestry, Inc. We have to squeeze past the heavy equipment before we can get close enough to see where Granny is spending her weekend.

The Ladies of the Forest have sure been busy. In stark contrast to the relentless grey of the rest of Tarragon Island, the camp is ablaze with colour. Orange flags, banners decorated with blood-red letters like the one they made at our house, bright blue tents, yellow rain slickers, and an array of umbrellas paint startling splashes of colour against the muddy gravel road.

Right in the middle of the road is a huge steel drum, the kind you see in the movies that gets rolled toward bad guys during car chases. This one is open at the top and a cheery fire blazes away inside, so hot it outcompetes the downpour. A kettle steams on a heavy mesh grate resting over the opening. Several women stand around the barrel, wiggling their hands over the flames.

Others, including Granny, have linked hands across the road and are singing as they sway back and forth in front of the first of the BIFI vehicles. Inside, an angry-looking man talks into his cellphone. He has covered his other ear with his hand, to drown out the singing, I guess, and moves only occasionally to gesture at the scene before him as if whoever it is on the other end might be able to see what is going on.

My heart pumps faster. What will happen if he gets tired of sitting in his truck, waiting for the women to go home? What if he starts it up and drives right over them?

The women don't seem too worried about this prospect. When one song finishes, they start singing another.

"Come on, Dad," Matt says. "There's Jennifer Lalli."

Matt can't wave because his hands are still full of food for the protesters, but he nods in the direction of one of the older women beside the garbage barrel.

"Matthew!" Mrs. Lalli shouts, her voice much larger than I would have expected for a woman her size. Mrs. Lalli is one of those tiny old women with extremely poofy hair and big glasses. Not that I can see her hair today. She, like many of the women, is wearing a knitted wool cap, the kind with earflaps that terminate in braided strings weighted down by a couple of pompoms.

Two people with video cameras film our approach. One of them is somebody I recognize from Granny's meetings at our house. The other one is Karin from the writing group.

I stop, turn around, and walk back toward the line of singing women. From this angle, the company truck looks huge. It's one of those big pickups that looks like a dump truck in disguise with monster wheels that hold the body of the truck way up high out of the mud, a grille on the front that looks like silver teeth, and a massive winch, maybe to haul other trucks out of creeks when they slide off the edges of the narrow planks they call bridges on these roads.

There's nowhere safe out here. I don't want to talk to Karin, but I sure don't want her to catch a tender moment between Granny and me, either.

"Heather?"

I turn and it takes me a minute to see where Dad's voice is coming from. Then I spot him under a kind of tarp awning the women have made in front of a massive tent that looks as if it could hold all of us and a truck or two as well.

Getting out of the rain sounds like one of the more sensible things to do under the circumstances, and I figure that Karin will find a bunch of dripping people hiding under a tarp a lot less interesting to film than the singers or the pyromaniacs, who are poking at the flames in the steel drum.

"Here."

I wrap my hands around the steaming mug of hot chocolate Dad hands me, purse my lips, and blow to cool it off. If there's one thing I can't stand, it's scalding the top of my tongue so it feels all weird and smooth and stops tasting things properly.

I take a sip. "Good," I say. And it is good. I settle myself into a folding chair toward the back of the covered area to wait until Dad and Matt have said their hellos and goodbyes and we can go home again. I would never admit it, but I'm kind of glad that Dad made me come to see the camp. I couldn't have imagined such a muddy, miserable, cold place to hang out. And it is sort of exciting and scary to see those women standing in front of the trucks, challenging those big guys and their equipment. It really is a kind of war in our very own woods.

Lots of writers have been inspired to write about wars. George Orwell wrote about the Spanish Civil War and Hemingway wrote stuff about the First World War and so did Timothy Findley. Some people make up their own wars to write about. Bunny, the lady at the bookstore, recommended I read John Marsden's war novels about teenagers who survive an invasion of Australia. I couldn't turn the pages fast enough to find out what bridges those kids were going to blow up next.

Maybe I could write something about this war, though to make it seem real I'd pretty well have to get right out in the trenches. I'd feel like a spy—or a liar—if I were to spend time in the woods with the protesters, pretending to be one of them only so I could write about what they were doing.

I watch the group that is still outside in the downpour. They haven't gone very far. A couple of the women have moved away from the fire and traded places with women in the singing group. Someone else emerges from a tent and Karin moves over to film her as she walks off down a trail and into the woods. Karin has the handle of an umbrella wedged between her cheek and her shoulder to protect the video camera as she works.

We stay for maybe half an hour until my hot chocolate is long gone and I'm shivering, despite the thick Cowichan sweater someone called Ivy lent me.

"We'd better get back," Dad says, and Granny gives him a big hug.

"Thanks for bringing the kids out," she says.

"When will you be coming home?" Dad asks.

"Probably tomorrow night. Monday morning at the latest. Some new recruits from Victoria are coming over to help us out. I wouldn't mind a long, hot shower!"

"I bet. Good luck!"

It's not as if I want to stay a minute longer than I have to or anything, but all the way back to the car I keep turning around to see if anything exciting is going to happen. But nothing does. The guy who had been yakking on his cellphone is still in his truck, but now his arms are folded over his chest and he just stares straight ahead, as if he can't even see the women on the road in front of him.

6

You can't try to do things; you simply must do them.

— Ray Bradbury

"Heather? Are you in there?"

Dumb question. Who else would be shivering out in Dove Cottage, writing? And who else but Alyssum would be bothering me?

"Hi, Alyssum. Come in."

Alyssum flings the door open and slams it behind her. I restrain myself from shushing her. She flops down onto the beanbag chair and pulls the thick quilt that's covering it around her. "Cold in here!"

I nod. There's no need to encourage Alyssum. She'll tell me what she wants without any help.

"Are you coming on Wednesday?"

It takes me a minute to figure out what she's talking about. "Is it the last Wednesday already?"

"Yup. It doesn't surprise me that you don't know that because you haven't exactly been helping me get ready for the meeting. Have you?"

I should have pretended I wasn't in here when she

knocked at the door. "How are the plans coming along? What are we going to be doing?"

"You are coming, then?"

"I guess so."

Alyssum and I started the Tarragon Island Kids Helping Kids Klub not long after I moved here last summer. We try to meet on the last Wednesday of each month, though we've managed to miss several meetings already what with Christmas and various family emergencies. Our group resolution this year is to meet regularly—no matter what.

"Matt wants to come," she says. It's a little strange I have to find out from my neighbour what my own brother is doing.

"He does? He never said anything about it to me."

"That's okay, isn't it? I told him he could."

What am I supposed to say to that? There isn't a good reason for him not to be able to join. It's not as if I'm crazy about the club at the moment. I've got enough other things to worry about.

"Did you know that 22 percent of Canadians basically can't read?"

"What?"

"It's true. And another 25 percent or so can only read simple stuff."

"In Canada? Are you sure?"

Alyssum nods and jiggles her feet up and down. "Positive. I read the statistics on the Internet."

"Wow. That's hard to believe." I try to imagine not being able to read. How could my eyes possibly focus on a word and not understand it? I read cereal boxes, road signs, the backs of tickets, menus, even the ludicrous instructions on bars of soap. (Wet hands. Rub soap between hands. Rinse.) Then I think about what effect not being able to read might have on my life. What kind of job can you get if you can't read?

"We could do something about that, though. We could do some kind of project to help people learn how to read."

"You mean, tutor kids or something?"

"And old people."

"Old people?"

"Yeah. Quite a few old people never finished school. Elementary school. So they have trouble filling out forms and stuff."

"But our group is about Kids Helping Kids."

Alyssum scrunches up her nose. "True. We could start another club—"

"No. Not a club that I have anything to do with. I'm already too busy as it is."

"I can see that."

I wave my pen at Alyssum but she's oblivious.

"You of all people should know that reading is important—"

"I didn't say it isn't." What would a writer like me do for a living if nobody knew how to read? "I can't believe that many people can't read—in Canada!"

"It's even worse in some other countries. Did you know that in Afghanistan lots of people, especially women and girls, don't have any books at all? No libraries to go to . . ."

It is impossible to listen to Alyssum for long without getting caught up in her enthusiasm. "We could collect books and send them to Afghanistan," I hear myself say as if some tendril from Alyssum has invaded my brain and is directing my lips and tongue. *Mental note: possible horror story plot.*

"They'd be in English, though," she counters. "And I don't think you can buy books in Afghani, or whatever they talk there, over here in Canada."

"Oh. Right."

"But we could raise money—maybe do a read-a-thon here and send the money we raise to someone who can get good books to people in other countries that don't have any."

"That's a good idea. A read-a-thon."

"I know. What can I say? I'm an idea factory."

I ball up a piece of paper and throw it at Alyssum. She squeals and wraps the covers around her head. From underneath the quilted lump her voice is muffled and giggly. "So, I take it this means you are coming to the meeting with tons of your usual enthusiasm?"

She does this to me every time, sucks me into her crazy save-the-world plans.

I don't answer. I don't have to—she knows I'll be there.

"I wonder who that could be?" Mom says, getting up from the dinner table.

We're used to getting emergency calls at all hours of the day and night, but it's Saturday evening and this call isn't coming in on the vet clinic line. It's on the house line.

"Probably another survey," Matt says, smearing a glob of butter onto his baked potato.

Recently, we've been getting a lot of calls from companies pretending to be interested in our TV viewing habits, or the number of computers we have in the house, or how often we vacuum, but really they're just trying to sell us stuff. They're not stupid, these people. They often call while we're all nicely gathered at home, eating dinner.

"Hello?" Mom is barely polite. I can tell she is ready to say something about how this call is invading her privacy and I'm sort of looking forward to the argument when she insists she get taken off the call list. She read somewhere about how they have to do it if you ask them to, but obviously they are never that enthused about cooperating with her request.

"Oh. I see. When did this happen?"

We've all stopped eating and Dad has turned around in his chair as if by watching Mom as she talks he'll be able to figure out who's on the other end of the line.

"Was she hurt?"

"Who?" Matt whispers.

"How long will she be there?"

"Who?"

Dad waves his hand at Matt to be quiet.

"I see. We'll wait for a call. Yes. Thank you."

Mom hangs up and when she turns around she has the strangest look on her face—a mix of disbelief, shock, and something else—irritation, maybe.

"So? Who was that?" Dad asks.

"That was Corporal Schofield."

"The police? Why are the police calling?" Matt asks.

Mom sighs. "Your grandmother has been arrested."

"What!" We don't even stop to laugh or "jinx" each other, even though we all shouted in unison.

"Granny's in jail?" Matt drops his fork.

"What happened?" Dad asks.

"Apparently several of the protestors refused to move off the road even when the police came and they were arrested."

"Granny is in jail?" I can't believe it. "It's illegal to stand on a road?"

"How long will she be there? Will they feed her?"

"Of course they'll feed her, dummy. This isn't the Middle Ages."

Matt scowls at me.

"Heather. That's enough. Since this is her first offence, it sounds as if they'll let her out in the morning."

"That's good news, I suppose," Dad says.

Mom sits back down. When she picks up her napkin her hands are shaking. "Maybe this will teach her a lesson. Maybe she'll stay at home and write letters to the politicians in Victoria."

"I think they tried that already—"

Mom silences Dad with a wicked glare. "They can try again. There's no need to get a criminal record for the sake of a few trees."

I look down at my peas and carefully load a few onto the tines of my fork. For once, I agree with my mother.

Letter writing seems like a good, safe strategy. Unfortunately, I already know that Granny doesn't see things that way.

Deciding how to retrieve Granny from the clink the next day leads to a huge fight. Mom has enormous bags under her eyes and doesn't move far from the coffee pot.

"No, Matt. I don't want to take you. I want to talk to your grandmother alone."

Dad intervenes on Matt's behalf. "Bobbi—what harm is there in letting him come along for the ride? He's going to see her soon—"

Another beady glare from Mom and Dad slams his mug down on the counter. "We didn't raise our kids to be sheep, did we?"

"We didn't raise them to be criminals, either!"

"I'm not a criminal!"

Mom ignores Matt's outburst and says, "My mother is not the kind of influence I want for my children."

"I have to disagree, Bobbi. What better role model do you want for them than someone who stands up for her rights and—"

"Ben. Enough. I don't think we should discuss this any further in front of the children."

Matt and I look at each other. I can't remember the last time I heard our parents argue like this. It's practically a full-out fight.

"I think they have every right to hear this—"

The clinic line rings and Mom's vet reflexes kick in.

She grabs the phone, asks a few questions, shakes her head, makes a note, hangs up, and then turns back to us.

"Mr. Hamber's mare is down again. I could be a couple of hours. Ben, please pick my mother up from jail and don't even think about taking the children."

Dad starts to protest but Mom is already sprinting down the hall to the clinic.

"Hey, Mattie. Don't cry."

Matt doesn't move, but he doesn't pull away when Dad puts his long arms around him and gives him a hug.

"But I-I-I want to see Granny. I want to come with you to pick h-h-er up."

"Wipe your nose," Dad says, handing him a tissue. "I don't think that would be a good idea."

They both look down the hall where Mom disappeared and Matt starts crying in earnest again.

"You want to come in my room to wait?" I offer. Dad gives me a little nod. "We could play some cards."

Matt sniffles. "Or you could teach me another card trick."

"I won't be long, Mattie," Dad says. "You can see Granny just as soon as I get back. Be good."

As he drives away it strikes me funny that he would tell us to be good. We aren't the ones being bailed out of the slammer.

We play Go Fish for a while and then I try to teach Matt a card trick about jacks going up and down an elevator but I can't remember the last part so it never works out quite right.

"How come Dad's taking so long?" he asks after more than an hour.

I shrug. "Maybe they stopped in town to pick something up."

"Can you read to me?"

Matt doesn't read very well, but he loves it when someone reads to him. I feel so bad for him I agree without even extracting a good trade. Usually I can get him to dry dishes for me or do my share of the dog runs out in the boarding kennels for a day or two in exchange for a chapter.

"What do you want to hear?"

"The Lion, the Witch, and the Wardrobe."

I don't even know why I bother to ask. He always asks for that book. He loves it almost as much as I do.

"Skip the first chapter," he says. "Just go to the part where Lucy is talking to Mr. Tumnus."

Matt knows the whole book pretty well off by heart. I turn to chapter two and start to read.

7

A writer doesn't solve problems. He allows them to emerge. — Friedrich Dürrenmatt

When Granny finally arrives home, Matt thunders down the stairs and barrels into her nearly hard enough to bowl her over.

"Matt! My goodness, what a welcome!"

Matt doesn't say anything, just buries his head in her stomach and lets her crush him in a mighty hug.

"Hi, Granny." I want her to know that I will still speak to her even though she has done time behind bars.

"Good to see you, love."

"Matt, let go of your grandmother. Let her sit down and have a cup of tea."

"No tea in jail," Granny says. "They kept offering us this dreadful coffee in Styrofoam cups. Hideous. They didn't have real milk—just that nasty powdered stuff."

"What was it like in jail? Were there murderers in there?"

Granny laughs. "This is Tarragon Island, thank goodness. There wasn't anyone there but protesters. It was a bit crowded. I don't think they're used to having twelve people in that little cell."

"You were all in one cell? Did you all get beds?"

"Beds? I'm afraid not. We took turns lying down on the concrete shelf, but I don't think anyone slept. It was too exciting! I've never been in jail before."

It's hard to know how she feels about her experience. She sounds a bit shocked but also pleased with herself. The minute she sits down in the armchair in the living room it is obvious just how tired she is. She slumps there, her arms out to the side, slung over the arms of the chair. Her hair is a mess, as if she hasn't slept all night or had a shower for days—both of which, I realize, are probably true.

"So, tell us all about it," Dad says. "What happened?"

She takes the cup of tea he offers and heaves a huge sigh. "It's a mess," she says. "They aren't going to give up easily. The trucks started moving, actually pushing us out of the way. That's when the police stepped in. Someone must have called them to say there was going to be trouble because they showed up just before the pushing started. I was singing and singing with my eyes closed the whole time. I couldn't believe those men would threaten to drive right over us! They could have killed someone!"

Granny gets more and more angry as she describes how the protesters sang louder and louder and the men in the trucks leaned on their horns and shouted obscenities at them. "So there we were, just regular citizens trying to do the right thing and protect those lovely ancient trees—for you, Heather, and you, Matt—and all the other grandchildren out there who will never see trees if we don't—"

"It's okay. You don't have to talk about this now." Dad pats her arm and I'm shocked to see that Granny's eyes are glistening. This is not some sort of prank. She really cares what happens to those trees.

"The children need to know, Ben."

Dad takes a deep breath as if he's going to argue but then he nods and she continues.

"When the trucks started rolling forward, so close they were touching us, so close I could feel the heat coming out of the engine, I knew that I had no choice but to stand up to them."

"Weren't you scared?" Matt asked.

"Terrified. So scared I thought I would scream. But I didn't scream. I kept singing and linked arms with the other women."

"What happened?"

"The police stepped forward. Four of them. I didn't even know there were that many officers here on the island. They asked us if we knew that we were breaking the law, that there was an injunction that said we were not allowed to be on the road any more."

"Why didn't they let you get off the road? Why did they take you to jail?"

Granny looks at me as if I have missed the whole point of her story. "They would have let us get off the road."

"Then they wouldn't have arrested you?"

"I don't think so."

"So why didn't you just move?"

"Heather, what those forestry companies are doing is wrong. If I have to go to jail to draw some attention to what is going on, then that's what I have to do."

"But it's their job to cut down trees."

"Not *those* trees, Heather. Those trees are some of the only giants left on the island."

"Don't you know the difference between old-growth and second-growth forests?" Matt asks as he crawls into Granny's lap.

"Of course she does, Mattie."

Truthfully? I don't particularly care that one tree isn't the same as another. But it hardly seems the time to point that out.

"Granny?"

"Yes, Heather?"

"What happened when you were all taken to jail?"

"I was in the back seat of the police car—with handcuffs on—"

"Handcuffs? How did you do up your seat belt?"

"No seat belts, Matt. No seat, really, just a hard bench behind a kind of screen divider—to keep the police officers safe, I suppose. Anyway, I couldn't see too much, but it looked as though an officer waved the trucks through as we were being driven away. The BIFI trucks drove past the camp and went back to work."

I'm almost sorry I asked because it looks as if she's going to start crying. But something in me keeps pushing, pressing forward, because I have a feeling this is my chance to make her see that making a fool of herself and getting arrested is not helping anything at all. Something else is happening, too. Writer Girl is waking up. She wants the whole story, even if I don't.

"So, all your camping out in the rain didn't work, did it?"

She looks at me gravely and slowly shakes her head.

"That, my dear, is why I have to go back."

When she says that, I want to throw something at her. I can't believe she is being so completely stupid. Grandmothers are not supposed to be stupid.

Matt throws his skinny arms around her neck and sobs. Maybe that will convince her to stay home with her family. She strokes his hair and tuts soothingly. "Shh, my darling. What can they do to me? I'm an old lady. They don't really want to keep me locked up. It will make them all look bad."

Matt snuffles and cuddles deeper into her arms. I wait for Dad to say something, but he is watching the two of them as though he can see something I can't. I don't think I've ever seen him with such a grim, tender expression on his face. That's when I know that the war in the Tarragon Woods is a long way from over.

8

They're fancy talkers about themselves, writers. If I had
to give young writers advice, I would say don't listen to
writers talk about writing or themselves. – Lillian Hellman

Mornings are not my best time of day. I know that some
authors get up really, really early and then write novels
until the sun comes up. I find that hard to believe. Maybe
people say stuff like that to impress their biographers. Or
maybe they have relatives they need to get away from.

Monday mornings are the worst of all. The day after
Granny gets out of jail, I wake up before anybody else.
Even Mia doesn't come out of Matt's room when I sneak
downstairs to get myself a bowl of cereal.

It's a strange feeling to be the only one awake in a
house full of sleeping people. The quiet isn't the same
kind of quiet as when you're really alone—like when I'm
out in Dove Cottage. It's more like an unnatural quiet
filled with slow breathing that you can't quite hear but
feel as if you should be part of. So it's lonelier, even
though I know that if I shout or drop something people

would appear—groggy, grumpy, confused people scrubbing crusty stuff out of the corners of their eyes, but people all the same.

It's ridiculous, but when I stare at the milk left in the bottom of the bowl wondering whether to tackle it with my spoon or just lift the bowl and drink it, I'm overwhelmed with a terrible aching sadness and I have to rush to the sink and tip the dregs down the drain so I won't start crying.

I plunk the bowl into the sink, hoping the clatter will get the day going, startle everyone else into wakefulness. No luck. Somewhere outside, even though it's still dark, I hear Tiny Tim, the Cranwells' bantam rooster, crowing. Tiny Tim is one of those weird rare breeds of chickens that looks like one of the Beatles from the 1960s, long hair flopping into his eyes. Long feathers, technically, but it really looks like a terrible haircut.

I spend almost another hour back up in my room reading about how Charles Dickens wrote and sold his novels in short sections that were published every few weeks so people without a lot of money could afford to read them. I'm the kind of person who likes to disappear into a novel and read it in one long sitting. I couldn't bear having to wait a year and a half to find out what's going to happen in the new Harry Potter book; reading it in pieces like a comic strip would kill me.

And what if Dickens changed his mind about something in the early part of the book by the time he got to the end? Unfortunately, what I'm reading doesn't really explain how he managed that part of things; whether later, when the books were published as novels all in one piece, he was allowed to go back and fix things up, make changes.

I find this omission strange. Every book I have ever read about writing novels includes stuff about how to do revisions. Rewrite, they say. Throw stuff out that isn't working. Personally, I find that hard, especially since a lot of those books say that some of your fanciest writing, the paragraphs with the most amazing, complicated, beautiful sentences with all the glorious, extra-interesting words are the ones you should probably cut out first since what really matters is getting to the point and telling the story rather than showing off how many big words you know.

Which reminds me that I haven't done a word list all week. I like to think of a word, anything that pops into my head, even if it's one I don't really understand. Then I write it down and add all the other words that are associated with it in any way. I use my dictionary and thesaurus and sometimes I can fill two whole pages with interconnected words.

I turn to a fresh page in my journal and the word that comes out of my pen is ANARCHY.

ANARCHY: Disorder esp. political or social . . .

ANARCHISM : The doctrine that all government should be abolished . . .

ABOLISH: Put an end to the existence or practice of (esp. a custom or institution).

ANARCHIST: An advocate of anarchism or of political disorder.

DISORDER: Confusion, disarray; lack of order or regular arrangement; a disturbance or commotion, esp. a breach of public order.

CONFUSION:

I'm just starting to write the definition for CONFUSION when my door swings open and Dad says, "Are you up yet?" I nearly fall off my chair with fright.

Somehow, the time has moved to 7:30 and if I don't hurry up and get dressed, I'm going to be late for school. That's what happens, I guess, when your grandmother is an anarchist who wants to abolish logging by disturbing the regular arrangement of logging trucks on the road to the Tarragon Woods which, in turn, creates confusion in the minds of everyone around her.

During my second breakfast, Granny sits opposite me and pours herself a cup of tea from the big pot in the middle of the table.

"Are you all right, Heather?" she asks.

I shrug. What am I supposed to say? I know she's really asking, "Do you still hate me?" Of course I don't exactly hate my grandmother, but I can't say I'm entirely happy with her, either.

"I'm fine. But I have to get to school. I've got a project due and I want to go to the library."

Dad looks at me, then at his watch and scowls. "Are you saying you want to go in early?"

"I guess so."

"Heather, if you suddenly change your plans, don't you think it would be courteous to let me know, since I'm the one who has to drive you?"

"I could take you in," Granny says.

"Never mind. Just never mind. I didn't think it would be a big deal. I'll go with Dad at the regular time."

"I'm standing right here, Heather," Granny says, reaching down for her muddy running shoes.

"Fine. I'll go with *you* at the regular time." Why does this always happen to me? I try to arrange things so I can get out of this house early so I don't have to fight with anyone and somehow this causes a bigger fight than if I'd just kept my mouth shut in the first place.

"Heather," Dad says. He's got himself under control and doesn't look quite so flushed. He takes a big swig of his tea and looks at his watch again. "It's not that I don't want to take you early—that's fine with me. It's just that I need a little warning if you are going to change plans on me. Okay?"

I nod and put a second empty bowl into the sink.

"So, give me ten minutes and then we can go."

"Thanks," I mumble, and sprint upstairs. What a mess. I'm not even ready to go. I throw my books into my backpack, tug a brush through my hair and twist my ponytail up into a messy bun. By the time I brush my teeth and run back downstairs again, Dad is already waiting outside in the truck.

9

Endless conflicts. Endless misunderstanding. All life is that. Great and little cannot understand one another.

— H. G. Wells

Standing in front of my locker, I wonder what on earth made me think I had to get to school early. Someone has painted a big warning on my locker with red paint.

YOUR FAMILY IS PIGS. LEAVE US ALONE.

There's no signature or anything, of course, and I just feel sick when I see it. Sick and scared and angry all at once. And the worst part is, part of me is really furious at Granny for getting me into this mess. At the same time, I feel scared for her. What if someone gets so mad at what she is doing that they come after her or set our house on fire or something?

"Heather?"

I whirl around. Mrs. Gurney, the principal, is standing right behind me. She reaches out for my shoulder but I pull back before she can touch me. I bump into my locker and jerk forward again as if I've been burned. I crane my neck around to see if any of the paint has rubbed off on my clothes.

"Heather, I'm sorry this has happened to you. Why don't you come to my office so we can have a chat?"

I'd love to be able to say no, but when the principal suggests you come to the office, the only thing to do is follow meekly and hope the meeting ends as soon as possible.

Mutely, I follow her down the hall, past the reception desk, and into her office.

"Have a seat," she says, and closes the door. She sits at her desk and picks up the phone to use the PA system.

"Mr. Purcell to the office, please. Mr. P to the office." Then she turns her attention back to me.

"That must have been a terrible shock, seeing that on your locker."

I nod.

"I know Mr. P is around—I saw him when I came in. I'll get him to clean off your locker—after we take some photos."

"Photos?"

"In case we are able to prosecute."

"Prosecute?"

She smiles sadly. "We don't take vandalism lightly. But I'd like to know—"

A knock at the door stops her and the janitor pokes his head in. Mrs. Gurney stands up and hands him a digital camera.

"Could you please take some photos of Heather Blake's locker—she's close to the gym doors—and then see what you can do about cleaning up that mess?"

When the door closes behind him, Mrs. Gurney says, "So, Heather. Do you have any idea what this is all about?"

I figure she probably knows very well what this is all about. Who on this island doesn't know about my grandmother? Why, I wonder, do grown-ups insist on doing that, asking a question to which they already know the answer? I guess Mrs. Gurney is trying to engage me in meaningful conversation. I don't feel like talking so I shrug.

"I read about your grandma," she says finally. "We have quite a few families at this school who rely on the forest industry for their incomes—not that this is an excuse for what happened to your locker," she adds hastily. "But it is understandable that there is a little . . . tension . . . here."

I stare down at her rug. It's quite beautiful, the type of thing you would expect to see in a fancy drawing-room in an old mansion in England or maybe at an Indian embassy. It has a rich, wine-coloured background with gold and black and yellow shot through it in an amazingly intricate pattern of diamonds and squares.

"That said, I don't think we can just let this incident pass without comment."

I stiffen. I don't want to know what's coming next, but Mrs. Gurney carries on, oblivious.

"I wanted to warn you that I will be calling a special assembly today. I'd like to speak about respect for other people's property and tolerance for other ideological positions. Heather? Do you understand what I mean by that?"

I nod. IDEOLOGY is a word in my collection. *A political or social philosophy.* I don't think I have a political or social philosophy except maybe "Everyone should leave Heather alone." Why can't she just wash my locker and be done with it?

"I don't think anyone is likely to step forward and admit to being the perpetrator, but I want to make it clear that this kind of behaviour will not be tolerated."

Her voice softens and she adds, "I wanted to let you know ahead of time so you wouldn't be too upset in the assembly. I won't mention your name."

"Thank you." I look longingly at the door.

"You may go in just a minute, but Heather . . ." She looks at me expectantly.

"Yes?"

"I want you to promise me that if there is any more trouble, if anyone threatens you or . . . anything happens that makes you uncomfortable, you will come and see me so we can take care of it."

I know she won't let me go until I agree so I nod. "I will." But as I walk back down the hall to my locker, where Mr. Purcell is busily scrubbing away at the word "PIGS," I know that someone would have to kill me before I would go and talk to Mrs. Gurney. And, of course, if I were dead, I'd have trouble sitting in the chair reserved for bad kids and victims of senseless crimes.

I don't think I have ever been happier to slip into my desk in Mr. McGuire's math class. I even find myself wishing that he'll keep giving us more and more examples of dividing fractions so I never have to leave the security of being under his watchful eye. That's when I realize just how horrible my life has become.

Assembly is just as bad as I fear it will be. Mrs. Gurney is so serious you would think someone had been murdered in the hallway.

"In a small community like ours, we cannot tolerate such behaviour."

Unfortunately, the more serious she gets, the more it makes me want to giggle. I'm not the only one. Two of the girls beside me snigger and Emma gives Terri a good shove. This makes her topple sideways and then Su says, "Hey—we can't tolerate that behaviour!" just loudly enough that Mrs. Gurney stops her speech but can't seem to tell exactly where the comment came from.

The whole assembly takes a turn for the worse and giggles and rude comments ripple through the crowd just ahead of or behind Mrs. Gurney's roving glare.

"That will be quite enough!" she says, and a reluctant silence fills the gym. "It may be a bit much to ask, but I'm going to do it anyway. If the person or persons responsible will voluntarily come to my office to discuss the matter of vandalism, I'm sure we can negotiate a fair resolution to this incident."

Sometimes she talks like such a principal. What exactly does "negotiate a fair resolution" mean? Community service instead of a public flogging? Needless to say nobody steps forward to make a weepy confession and I doubt she'll be overwhelmed by visitors to her office, either.

Mrs. Gurney folds her arms across her chest and peers at us over her glasses. "I know that you know the difference between right and wrong. I trust you will all make an effort to make better choices in the future."

With a nod to our homeroom teachers, we are dismissed. It's pretty obvious that the staff have all been briefed, because when we go back to homeroom Mrs. Stukus repeats a lot of the stuff Mrs. Gurney said in assembly about taking personal responsibility for our actions, talking out our frustrations, and taking vandalism seriously.

When she asks if anyone has anything to add, the only person to put up her hand is Steffie, who asks, "Do we still get morning break?"

Mrs. Stukus rolls her eyes and sits down behind her desk. I sit over near the windows and I wonder if it's a coincidence that Mrs. Stukus never once looks over in my direction.

If possible, things get worse from there. I had no idea that paranoia is so exhausting. For the rest of the day it seems that kids are either staring at me or avoiding me or whispering things as I pass in the halls. Even though nobody actually does anything that I could call rude or threatening, the turmoil in my stomach gets worse and worse until the last class finally grinds to an end and I flee the building, sloshing my way through the puddles to the school bus.

10

Alone, alone, all, all alone,
Alone on a wide wide sea!
And never a saint took pity on
My soul in agony.
> – Samuel Taylor Coleridge,
> "The Rime of the Ancient Mariner"

I stay in my room most of the next day even though there's school. Dad believes me when I say I have a horrible headache. And that's not a complete lie because my head is full of nasty visions of my locker and the leering ball cap kids. I have a kind of psychological headache.

Psychological or not, I know enough to come downstairs just after lunch to let them know I'm starting to feel better and that my appetite is coming back. In truth, I'm about ready to faint from starvation, but I can't admit to that or they will know I haven't been exactly honest about my reason for staying home.

"You need more sleep, Heather," Granny says. Sleep deprivation is her standard explanation for any sign of illness. That, and a lack of fresh vegetables. According to

Granny, if everyone got enough sleep and ate plenty of fruit, salad, and bran cereals we wouldn't need doctors any more.

So I tell her I'm going to have a nap, but really I lie on my bed and go on reading a novel by Dennis Foon called *Skud*. It's about these four teenagers, all boys, whose lives are intertwined in some way. The whole book is written in the first person, but all four boys have their own chapters. So, one chapter is called *Tommy* and the next one *Shane* and then maybe *Brad* takes a turn. You would think it would get confusing, but it doesn't. I feel that I'm getting to know these kids, that they are talking to me. Maybe that's because Dennis Foon writes good dialogue so it feels as though the characters are based on real people.

Reading *Skud*, I get inspired to try to write something in that style, using alternating narrative voices.

SOPHIA

Nothing my family can say will change my mind about saving the trees.

Gunfire crackles through the forest beyond the circle of light thrown from the windows of my log cabin.

"Sophia!" Someone thumps on the door so loudly the cat scuttles under the couch, eyes wide, tail puffed out like the tail on a coonskin cap.

"Who is it? What's happening?"

The door flies open and my granddaughter falls inside. "Grandmother!" She is sobbing and I feel her small body crumple into my arms.

"Felicia. What are you doing here? Why did you run so far in the dark? What will your mother and father say? They will be angry and they will be worried."

My granddaughter Felicia wails, "Oh Grandmother! I had to come even though I was scared because I had to warn you! Some men with guns are coming this way and you are in danger for your life!"

I read this over and want to puke. How does Dennis Foon do it? His characters sound as if they are really having conversations. Mine sound like bozos. No kid would say, "You are in danger for your life!" And no child would call her grandmother by her first name.

I scratch out *Sophia!* And replace it with *Grandmother!* But then the next line doesn't make sense because obviously a grandchild is at the door and even if Sophia has a bunch of grandchildren she wouldn't say, "Who is it?" She'd open the door and let the poor kid in, especially if there are gunshots ringing through the forest.

The urge to crumple the page and toss it into the trash is pretty strong. But Ms. Thompsen, our English teacher, wouldn't approve. She's one of those teachers who is very big on the creative process. At first, I didn't really think she would be able to teach me too much about that—I am working on a novel and I've written tons of poems and I live with a painter—but Ms. Thompsen's approach is kind of cool. She likes to use messy brainstorming, connecting things in circles with lines and arrows and making lists and that sort of thing. Her philosophy on first drafts is Never Erase. Instead, she says it's important to just blurt everything onto the page, good, bad, or otherwise. Later, when we are revising, that's when we get rid of dumb stuff or flesh out "thin scenes," as she calls them.

So, I leave in all the bad dialogue and the illogical part of the scene and put a star in the margin to remind me that I might want to reconsider. Another thing Ms. Thompsen does is make us do at least three sets of revisions. Sometimes I cheat just a little and do one set but then print off three copies of my first draft and spread all the changes around a little. I don't think she even looks at the in-between stages, so all that really matters is that the final draft is okay. So far, anyway, my method seems to be working fine because she hasn't deducted marks for my not-quite-accurate revisions.

The bigger problem, though, has nothing to do with bad dialogue and shaky logic. What I really can't get my head around is why the grandmother would put herself and her family at risk over some trees. Without understanding *that* (another thing Ms. Thompsen is pretty big on is character motivation), I don't think anyone is going to understand the story. How could they when I don't understand it myself?

Between writing (and trying really hard not to revise) my new multi-narrator story (that has only one narrator so far) and reading bits and pieces of *Skud*, the rest of the day goes really fast.

The next day at school I retreat to the library during breaks and at lunchtime, and manage to avoid everybody except Eric, who is researching strange things that people collect for a character in the mystery story he's working on for TWYG. He shows me a picture of this guy in a trucker's cap leaning up against a monster ball of twine. According to the listing in a *Ripley's Believe It or Not!* book, the ball took forty years to make and lived in this guy's yard chained to a tree.

"Chained to a tree? What kind of moron would want to steal that?"

"Who could lift it?" Eric asks. "Who would want to steal it? Why? And then what would they do with it?"

Eric's mystery-writer wheels are spinning at hyperspeed, I can tell. He leans over the photo and says, "There—you can see the chain in the background. Why wouldn't someone just cut the string to get it free?"

"Maybe the chain was put on way inside the ball, before he added the last, say ten thousand layers."

Eric nods. "That makes sense. Back when the guy added the chain, the ball might have been small enough to lift."

Before Eric can say anything about the vandalism incident or ask why I'm in the library, I find a table and pull out my notebook, math textbook (in case a teacher comes past), and *Skud*. I write another page of my story, this time from the point of view of Felicia, the granddaughter. It's a little easier to write her part because I can kind of understand why a child would want to save her dear grandmother from snipers. But I still can't figure out why her grandmother would put her family in danger in the first place. I might have to take it to read at the writing group tomorrow night—maybe the others will have some good suggestions.

11

The decline of literature indicates the decline of a nation.
— Johann Wolfgang von Goethe

Matt and I talk about the meeting of the Kids Klub over supper. Matt and Alyssum have been plotting and scheming together all day. That's one of the advantages of schooling at home—you can apply your energy in the places where your interests lie. (That's a quote right out of the Cranwells' philosophy book.)

I had plenty of time during my self-inflicted exile to come up with a few ideas of my own about what we could do to help more people read better. Now it strikes me that Matt is one of the 40-whatever percent of Canadians who have trouble reading. I wonder how many of the people who have trouble reading have dyslexia, like Matt?

"We're going to help kids right here on the island," Matt explains, peas dribbling out of his mouth.

"Matt! Chew. Swallow. Talk. In that order, please," Dad says, though not terribly fiercely.

"Reading?" Mom asks. "Your club is going to teach

other kids to read?"

Something in the tilt of her head and her cocked eyebrow says that she thinks it's crazy to expect that Matt could help anybody read anything. It's not meanness, I know that. But sometimes, when she tries to protect him, I think that hurts more than speaking up about whatever is bothering her.

Matt picks up the unspoken message, too. I can tell because after he swallows he doesn't keep on talking the way he would have if Mom hadn't said anything. Instead, he slices off a strip of his pork chop, takes a bite, and chews very, very slowly as if he has all the time in the world and isn't in a rush to get over to Alyssum's after dinner. Granny winks at him but he either doesn't notice or ignores her.

"We all have different jobs," I say, hoping nobody asks what they are because we haven't been to the meeting yet, which is when we'll decide all that stuff. "Did you know that 22 percent of Canadians basically can't read?"

Dad's fork clinks against his plate. "That doesn't sound right to me."

"In Canada?" Granny says. "Are you sure?"

The statement is inflammatory enough that Mom and Dad have an argument or, as they would say, a spirited debate about illiteracy around the world. That slides off into general complaining about the state of our education system and how there's nobody decent to vote for in the next election. This gets Granny going about her theory that the government minister for environmental issues is being bribed by the forest companies.

As the spirited debate deteriorates into fists banging on the table (Granny), dismissive waves (Mom), and stares at the ceiling with puffed-out cheeks (Dad), Matt and I finish stacking the dishes by the sink and sneak off to our rooms to get sweaters and notebooks.

"See you later!" I call as Matt fumbles with the flashlight out on the back steps.

"Don't get lost!" Dad calls back. He always says that before we head next door. We all know it's not likely to happen, but every time Matt and I make the trek along the path we've cut through the trees between our place and the Cranwells', it feels as though we are embarking on a long and dangerous journey.

"Do you have plenty of supplies?" I ask Matt in my conquering Everest voice.

"Enough for seven days." This means Matt has packed seven cookies.

"Spiced with the healing cocoa bean?" I ask in code, hoping to find out what kind of cookie he's bringing. A branch whips back and stings my cheek. "Ow!"

"Sorry."

"Cocoa beans?" I repeat. "That really hurt!"

"Many beans to maximize available energy. I said sorry."

The bobbing flashlight beam catches something shiny and metallic just as the trees thin out and the ground starts to rise beneath our feet. We have arrived on the roof of the Cranwells' underground house: their shiny metal chimney is like a beacon to guide our way to base camp. This, and the fact Matt has brought chocolate-chip cookies, mitigate the irritation I'm still feeling about the branch smacking me in the face.

Damp pine needles give way to a path of glistening pebbles through the moss and grass of the roof. We follow the curve of the house and Matt snaps the flashlight off as we step around the back, blinking in the harsh glare of the patio light.

Slapping through the puddles, Matt runs over to Alyssum's French doors and pushes his face against the glass of one of the square panes. Inside, Alyssum shrieks and Matt hoots with laughter.

The door swings open and Alyssum tumbles out, giggling, her bare toes dancing on the flagstones awash with rainwater.

"Gotcha!!" Matt shouts.

I'm too old for this kind of nonsense, so I push past Matt and Alyssum and go inside.

"Hi."

The person sitting on the bed has the biggest, darkest eyes I have ever seen in my life—except maybe in a deer or a cow. They swallow the girl's whole face and I have to force myself to check to see whether she has lips and a nose to go along with them. Of course she does, but her whole face exists to frame those eyes.

"Hi. I'm Heather."

"I guessed that," she says. "I'm Uma."

"Hi." *Uma*? What kind of a name is Uma?

The mysterious Uma is lost inside a baggy pair of overalls and a bright red sweater, thick, warm, and probably homemade. I think she must be the quiet type, the way her eyes follow me into the room. A little strange, perhaps—like part lizard or cat—because her eyes don't blink.

Caught in the alien's dissecting beam, Writer Girl breaks out in a sweat. She notes her alternatives: run back out the way she came in—not an alternative because the other aliens are right behind her—or keep going right through the cluttered alien headquarters and into the underground tunnel beyond—not a good option either because the Mama alien and her twin offspring lurk out there. Writer Girl turns to stare back at the dark-eyed alien, engages her in a staring competition. The winner will laugh, stomp on the loser's heart. The loser will lie bleeding on the ground, a useless lump of soulless flesh.

This, I think, is why people write comic books. It would be so much easier to write about the strangeness of this moment if I could draw a picture of those eyes, maybe draw a picture of Writer Girl being melted into a puddle by a stare.

"Did you meet Uma?" Alyssum asks. "Uma? Did you meet Heather?"

Uma nods and then picks a fluffball off the sleeve of her sweater.

"Uma home-schools, too. We met back when I was in cello class, before I started African drumming."

"Hi," I say for the third time. What a moron. I push aside a pile of books and sit at one end of Alyssum's big table. As usual, the entire surface of the table is covered with Alyssum's half-finished projects—a model that looks a bit like Shakespeare's Globe Theatre, a poster comparing different types of bird bills, complete with two actual beaks that Alyssum has attached to the cardboard with yellow ribbon, and a string of Christmas tree lights strung up between two branches and attached to a battery and something that resembles a big clothes peg.

Alyssum plops down on the only bare spot on her bed. "Mom and I went through my books and we found some that would be particularly good for helping kids read," she says, plunging right into the subject of our meeting.

It turns out that Uma isn't quiet at all. In fact, for the rest of the evening she is never again as quiet as she was during the first minute or so when all I could see were her dark, intense eyes. She, Alyssum, and Matt are soon arguing over which books would be best to use, which ones were boring, which ones a mother might like but which a kid, especially one who was having trouble reading, would hate. Matt has lots to contribute on that front. Mom and Dad and, in the old days, his teachers were forever trying to convince him that this book or that book would be good for him to read. But Matt likes to read books of lists and strange statistics, or magazines and Internet sites about taking care of animals, especially cows and sheep. If I read a novel like *The Lion, the Witch, and the Wardrobe* to him, he'll sit and listen while he draws or clips his cockatiels' toenails. At night, I often hear him falling asleep to the deep voice of a narrator who is reading a book on tape.

"It is so reading when you read a list," he argues with Uma. "How else could you possibly know what's on the list if you don't read the words?"

In the end, we decide that as long as the book is shaped like a book and has words in it, we can use it in our tutoring program. This debate takes nearly an hour and might have gone on even longer if Alyssum hadn't asked, "Hey, Mattie, did you bring any cookies?" I'm a little surprised that Matt lets Alyssum call him that. He generally hates it when people (other than Granny) call him anything other than plain old Matt.

We're all good and ready for a break. Mrs. Cranwell could have been waiting on the other side of the door because we have hardly had a chance to open the tinfoil package Matt pulls from his bag when she knocks and asks if we'd like some milk or juice.

"How are we going to find kids who need our help?" Uma asks after the drinks have been delivered.

"They must be everywhere," Alyssum says, "if that many people can't read. We could put up posters, like in the grocery store and at the laundromat . . ."

"But how would people read the signs if they can't read?"

"Good point," Alyssum concedes. "We could draw pictures and make the posters really simple, with not too many words. Friends or people in the family could read to them."

"We could phone the schools," Matt says, "and let the teachers know we can help kids."

"I can't come during school hours," I remind them. "What about you?"

Uma nods her head. "I can. Home-school, remember?"

"Oh, right. Well, that's great—you guys can go into

school during the day, I guess. I'll have to do my tutoring after school or on the weekends."

"You could write an article for the paper, couldn't you, Heather? You know Mr. Turnbull. You practically worked at the *Tarragon Times*, didn't you?"

I would hardly call the two articles I wrote last year a job, but Alyssum likes to exaggerate. "I guess I know him a little."

"So call him and ask him if you can write something about literacy to promote what our club is doing."

I have learned that there is no point in arguing with Alyssum. Chances are, the *Tarragon Times* won't even be interested in an article about kids reading to other kids, but on her to-do list, Alyssum puts my name beside Contact Local Media.

Before I know what's happening, I have also agreed to call the librarian at the elementary school and put up a poster at the high school to see if anyone else wants to be a reading tutor. Matt and Alyssum are going to make a big, colourful box where people can drop off books to donate for our tutoring program. We're all going to ask our parents if they have any fundraising ideas for money to buy books for kids overseas.

Alyssum and Uma practise reading to Matt and me, but Matt refuses to read aloud.

"I have to practise by myself first," he says, and I can tell he's thinking about the strange way Mom responded to our idea of being reading tutors.

"I'll help you, Matt," I say. "We have lots of good books at home."

"We can probably get some at the library, too," he says.

I nod, though I'm not sure how much luck we're going to have. The island library is kind of small and the children's section isn't very good. Dad says they don't have much of a budget, so they totally depend on people donating books and that means a lot of the kids' books are pretty old and have been well used before they ever make it onto the library shelves. Volunteers run the place and they are mostly old ladies who read Agatha Christie novels and romantic stories with cowboys on the cover. (Okay, that's a bit of an exaggeration, but not much. They do have lots of books on birdwatching, microwave cooking, and shipwrecks.) The hours are terrible, too: they're closed on Sundays and Mondays, and on the other days of the week are only open from two to five in the afternoon. Saturdays are a bit better. If you're looking for a good book you have from ten until three to choose one.

The Tarragon Island library is another reason I still sometimes miss Toronto. We do have cards for the Victoria library, but unless we know we are going to travel to Vancouver Island again within the month, we can't take out any books without racking up huge fines.

"Heather?"

"Huh?"

"I asked you about the date."

"What date?"

Alyssum pushes out her bottom lip. "You never listen to me."

"Yeah. She's probably writing another dumb poem in her head."

"Shut up, Matt. Sorry, Alyssum. What date?"

"The date when we can start our program. When do you think would be good?"

"How about right after spring break? That way we can sort of make our plans between now and the holiday, choose books and practise reading over the break, and be ready to start the week after that."

Uma nods. "Sounds good to me."

"Great!" Alyssum claps her hands. "Great meeting, guys. Thanks for coming over."

It's obvious we're being sent home.

"What about you?" Matt asks Uma.

"Uma is staying over tonight."

"Oh."

If I didn't know better, I would almost think Matt is a little bit jealous.

12

You may be able to take a break from writing, but you
won't be able to take a break from being a writer.

— Stephen Leigh

"When are you going to call the paper?" Matt asks as
we're walking back from the barn after the morning
chores on Thursday.

"If you ask me that one more time, I'm going to—"

"What?" Matt dances out of the way. "What are you
going to do? When are you going to—"

"Be quiet!" My teeth feel as though they're going to
grind their way right up into my brain.

"Well, when?"

"Now! Right now, if you'll shut your mouth!"

"You don't have to yell. You were the one who promised to call."

The look I give Matt must be sufficiently wither-
ing because he refrains from saying anything else. He
doesn't even follow me into the kitchen when I go to
make the call. Just my luck, Mr. Turnbull answers the
phone himself.

"*Tarragon Times*, good morning."

"Oh, hi, Mr. Turnbull. This is Heather Blake calling."

"Heather! Hello, how are you?" He doesn't even give me a chance to answer. "Isn't that funny—I was going to give you a call this week to ask you if you might consider submitting a story. And here you are, phoning right out of the blue."

"Thank you. I . . . I was calling about a story, too!"

"Wonderful!" He laughs and I can practically see his jowls wobbling, his pudgy fingers patting his ample tummy. "So, tell me—what do you have in mind?"

"Reading," I say, and then, into the hollow silence, I add, "Lots of people can't read very well so the Kids Klub that I started with Alyssum last year is going to raise money for poor libraries—or, well, libraries in poor countries—and then we're also going to be doing some tutoring for kids right here on the island who are having trouble with their reading—" The words bumble and tumble out, not at all like the prepared speech I was going to give complete with statistics. Throughout it all, there is absolute silence at the other end of the line. "So, I was thinking maybe you would be interested in a story about something like that."

Lame. Definitely lame. Not a professional-sounding conversation at all. I'm sure he thinks I'm just a dumb kid who can't string two words together. He probably thinks I didn't even write those other two articles myself.

"Interesting idea. I can't promise anything, but sure, see what you come up with and I'll have a look. But while I have you on the phone, I understand your grandmother is one of the Ladies of the Forest?"

My stomach plummets right down to my shoes. "Um, yes."

"That's what I thought. Was she one of the people who was arrested?"

I can tell by the way he asks that he already knows the answer. "Yes. She was."

"What's going on out there in the forest is a great story. Do you think you could write something about what your grandmother is up to? From the perspective of a family member? An insider?"

If he had asked me to write an article about castrating sheep, I would have been happier. "I'm not really an insider."

"You've been up to the blockade, haven't you?"

"Yes," I have to admit.

"And my wife tells me that some of the planning meetings are at your house—or have I got my facts wrong?"

"No. You're right. The Ladies of the Forest do come over here sometimes."

"And that is your grandmother knitting the long scarf in the December photograph of the calendar?"

"Yes. That's her."

"Well, you're as much an insider as anyone. We're going to be doing a whole section in the paper about the protests two weeks from now. Could you have something to me by the end of next week?"

For some reason the excuse-making part of my brain cannot think of a single reason not to meet the deadline. At least, no excuse that I could share with a virtual stranger. The words just burble out of my mouth almost as if Alyssum has moved back into my body and is moving my lips and tongue around again. "Sure. I can write something for you."

"Excellent! I'll look for two stories, then—one about your reading project and the other about the protests." In the background, another phone rings and rings. "I have to grab that other line, Heather. It's been great to hear from you!"

There's a click and then nothing. The silence is awful. Not a single word comes to me that might fill the horrible space.

"So? What did he say? Can you do a story?" Matt asks, crashing through the kitchen door.

I nod, slowly. "Two," I say and his eyes bulge out.

"Two? He wants two articles for the paper? About reading?"

I shake my head. "One about reading and one about . . . something else."

Matt hardly seems to hear. "Are you done with the phone? I have to call Alyssum! This is so great! We're going to raise tons of money and get hundreds and thousands of books and then a bunch of kids will get to be better readers and . . ."

He's still listing all the great things that are going to happen all because of the article I'm supposed to write when I leave the kitchen and head back outside and into the first, tentative drops of rain. Dove Cottage is cold and damp at this time of year, but at least it's quiet and I don't have to listen to what Matt might be saying on the phone.

13

Do not the most moving moments of our lives find us all without words? – Marcel Marceau

On Friday, Matt, Mia, Alyssum, and her hyperactive golden retriever, Sandy, are all waiting for me at the end of the driveway when I get off the school bus. Like a crazed army they charge toward me, yelling and barking. The bus takes its own sweet time to get going again, so everybody on the bus has plenty of opportunity to stare.

"What are you guys doing here?"

Sandy leaps up at me, her big paws jamming into my stomach and leaving two muddy footprints.

"Sandy! Get down!" Alyssum grabs Sandy's collar and hauls her backwards. "You mind your manners, you naughty dog."

Mia runs in circles, yapping and whining, and won't stop until I crouch down to pat her. Her entire dog body convulses with happy wiggles. It's impossible not to laugh when she cranes her neck and slobbers dog kisses all over my face and neck.

"What's this?" Matt asks, waving a postcard at me.

"Hold still. I can't see."

"It's for you," Alyssum said.

"If it's for me, why do you guys have it?" I snatch the postcard. The picture on the front shows the *Maid of the Mist* puttering toward the bottom of Niagara Falls. A pit opens inside me and I feel like I'm falling into it backwards. My mind whirls. Why does Matt have my postcard from Grandpa? "Don't touch my stuff!" I scream at him.

Matt and Alyssum look at each other and then back at the postcard in my hand. Even the dogs stop barking.

"My mom says that postcards aren't really private mail and that anyone who sends a postcard should expect they'll be read by other people—I mean, even if you aren't trying, your eyes see stuff . . ." Alyssum falters.

"I don't care what your mother says. You guys have no right to go into my room and take my things. This is *personal*." Tears burn and I gulp a deep breath so they don't spill over. "It's the last postcard Grandpa ever sent to me before . . . before he . . . "

"Heather," Matt says quickly. "This arrived today."

"Today?"

He reaches out, gently takes the card from me, and turns it over. "See?"

The writing on the back is not my grandfather's. Someone else has sent me the same card. "Oh. You still shouldn't have read it," I say, but my voice is flat, quiet. The anger has fizzled away. So has their enthusiasm.

"We just wanted to know what it means," Alyssum

says. "But you don't have to tell us. You're right. It's your mail."

"Do you want to go back to your house?" Matt asks. Alyssum nods and all four of them trot off down the driveway next to ours leaving me alone holding the post-card.

SEE YOU SUNDAY

See you Sunday? There's no signature. Nothing else. Everything, even my address, is in block letters. The handwriting seems vaguely familiar, but I can't place it. I turn the card over again. The *Maid of the Mist* is still there, half obscured by the clouds of spray kicked up by the gazillions of tons of water plunging over Niagara Falls.

Granny and Grandpa took us on that boat trip once. I was maybe ten and it was my first trip to Niagara Falls, even though we didn't live that far away, in Toronto. Grandpa had been before, and I remember he made us line up really early so we would be the first on board. We pushed right up to the bow of the boat, the four of us all dressed in these matching blue plastic rain ponchos. It was a really hot day and Matt wanted to take his off, but Granny wouldn't let him.

Everything was so loud—the rumble of the boat's engines, all the people shouting and screaming, and then the thundering water pounding against the rocks, into the water, all around us as though we were right inside the thudding heart of the water-sound. The falls were so loud we couldn't hear each other even when we yelled at the top of our lungs.

At first, the mist had been cool and pleasant and I thought it was a bit silly to be wearing those huge ponchos. But then, when the boat got closer, it felt as if we were in a hurricane or something. Water seemed to pour down on us and the noise was deafening. It seemed as if we were going to crash into the rocks, or be sucked under the falls, and we were all going to die. Just when I turned to Grandpa and screamed "I want to go back!" the boat eased off and let the current push her away from the tumult, and only a few minutes later we were back at the dock, tying up.

Then, both Matt and I wanted to go back out again but Grandpa said it was time for ice cream.

Thinking of his kind smile, the way he helped us out of our ponchos and then took our hands in his own big farmer's hands, thick and calloused, is too much for me. I haven't made it halfway up the driveway before tears drip down my cheeks. By the time I'm in the house, I'm practically drowning, half blind with misery. I run up to my room, slam the door, and throw myself on my bed clutching the postcard to my stomach and cry and cry and cry for the longest time.

I keep expecting Dad or Mom or even Granny to knock on the door to see what's wrong, but nobody does. Eventually I calm down enough to wash my face and brush my hair, two things Mom always says are guaranteed to make a person feel better after a good weep.

A good weep. Is there such a thing as a *good* weep? I can't say that I feel any better after mine, but maybe I would feel even worse if I didn't cry once in a while.

Damn Grandpa. Why did he have to go and die anyway? It happened last fall and it sometimes feels as if he's still dying. Or, even stranger, that he is still with me. Just when I think I'm pretty much over the shock of it, something happens and the agony of losing him floods back over me.

When Mom went to Ontario for the funeral, we didn't go with her. I never asked what Grandpa looked like in his coffin and Mom never offered any details. I guess she didn't want to traumatize me, but what actually happened was I started thinking that Grandpa was really alive, that he had faked his own death and run off with some model from New York.

In my fantasies, the two of them had bought a sailboat and were sailing around the world. After the whole family had forgiven him for leaving my grandmother, he was going to sail into Rosehip Harbour, call us up, invite us out for salmon and crab cakes down at the marina, and apologize for causing us all a lot of unnecessary grief. And now here's this card from Niagara Falls, and I have this crazy idea that he really isn't dead after all, that he's going to come and see me on Sunday. I pick it up and stare at the message, then unzip my backpack and pull out my calendar.

Sunday. There it is. A note to myself: *11 a.m. receive, 11:30 a.m. send.*

I look at the handwriting again and it's so obviously Maggie's that I can't imagine how I could have been confused, even for a minute. I'm not sure whether to laugh at Maggie for being such a goof, or at myself for thinking the card was from Grandpa.

I decide I'll go find some chocolate, something guaranteed to make me feel better in times of distress. Luckily, Matt made lots of cookies and froze some. I fish out one of the packages he left in the freezer and take it back up to my room. He sticks his frozen cookies into the microwave oven to soften them up a little before he eats them, but I like to munch on them in their frozen-solid state. There isn't anything better than frozen chocolate chips.

14

Every journalist who is not too stupid or too full of himself to notice what is going on knows that what he does is morally indefensible. He is a kind of confidence man, preying on people's vanity, ignorance, or loneliness, gaining their trust and betraying them without remorse.
— Janet Malcolm, "The Journalist and the Murderer"

"Heather?"

"What?"

"Could you please answer politely?"

Why should I be polite? I'm trying to work on my article and people keep interrupting me—first Matt, then a phone call from this girl at school who wanted to know if I could lend her my English notes, and now Dad.

"Yes, Father?"

The door opens and Dad sticks his head in. "Busy?"

The truthful answer would be, "Yes." Sensibly, I think, I do not say anything.

"Answer me! Honestly, Heather, I don't know what's got into you lately."

"I am working on my article for the newspaper." I measure out each syllable and deliver it carefully, precisely, politely.

He nods. I don't think he really cares one way or the other whether I'm writing an article or doing homework or creating another collage journal page. This is another annoying trait of grown-ups: asking questions when they don't even care about the answer. It's like they are trying to teach us the art of idle conversation, as if whatever we might be doing isn't as important or timeworthy as whatever it is they have in mind.

"I need a hand."

I feel my lip rising in a sneer and have to turn away so Dad doesn't notice. "Doing what?"

"Well, as a matter of fact, I don't need a hand. Your grandmother needs your help."

"Doing what?" I repeat, hoping I sound just a little bit interested and not too rude, or I know my dessert options will be severely restricted.

"Writing a press release."

I snort. I can't help it, the noise just whooshes out of me. "I don't know how to write a press release. I don't even know what a press release is, exactly." This is not quite true—we wrote press releases to announce the formation of our Kids Helping Kids Klub. That was a while ago, and I hope Dad doesn't remember.

"Of course you do. You wrote great press releases for your club. Remember?"

"Oh. Right. I guess so. But that was different. You know how people like stuff kids do because it's cute. They could have been terrible press releases and the paper still would have printed them."

Dad shakes his head. "I would disagree with you there. You guys were newsworthy. You're going to be newsworthy again, once you get your new project going. So, I am asking you a favour. Please talk to your grandmother and find out what she needs to let the world know about and then write a draft of the press release. She'll tell you if there are any changes and then she'll send copies to the papers and radio stations here, on Vancouver Island, the mainland . . ."

It's a fight to hold my tongue.

"You don't have to sigh like that. For heaven's sake, nobody's asking you to carry a sign out in the forest or do anything you might find embarrassing. Nobody even needs to know you helped out. It would mean a lot to your grandmother."

It turns out that Granny wants me to write a press release to announce a new logging road blockade. Grannies are coming from all over British Columbia to hold hands and sing at the logging trucks. There's even a vanload of old ladies who are coming up from somewhere near Seattle, Washington.

As I make notes about what the old ladies have planned, I stick to the five Ws, thinking that this will keep things simple. Hah! Granny makes changes to just about every single word.

WHO: *Ladies of the Forest* (Even this needs adjusting. Granny makes me add "and allies.") *A group of old women with bongo drums.* (Granny crosses this out and puts "concerned seniors and elders" instead, even though I think she is repeating herself.)

WHAT: *Radical act of disruptive civil disobedience.* (Granny doesn't like this, either. She says there is no need to alienate people and writes, "Peaceful protest with songs to celebrate our Mother Earth.")

WHEN: *High noon, Saturday, February 5.* (Granny crosses out "high" because she says it makes it sound like there is going to be a shootout on the logging road. Which—if she makes enough people mad—there just might be.)

WHERE: *Lower Tarragon Road, near the Kogawa cut-off.* (Miracle! No changes!)

WHY: *To get in the way of the logging trucks.* (Wrong again! This is what she writes instead: "Old-growth forests are not the same as tree farms. These trees belong to all of us, not just the logging companies. Come join us for a celebration of life and diversity!")

After I type all the changes and take them back down to Granny, she peers at me over her reading glasses and beams. "This is wonderful, Heather! Exactly what I wanted. Thank you! We should really do an information sheet, too."

"Information sheet? Isn't that what we just did?" The words spit out of my mouth. Granny explains the situation to me as if I were a little kid.

"We just created a wonderful press release. The information sheet will give those media people more details about the issues."

Writer Girl clicks out her retractable talon and drags the diamond tip underneath the words, "Old-growth forests are not the same as tree farms." *Isn't this the issue? Some trees are more worthy than others. As her claw moves across the page the words begin to smoke and she blinks as her eyes stare into the blue-green flame.*

"Right?"

"Sorry. What?"

"I said, not everyone understands how destructive some of our forestry practices are."

Granny gives a little nod toward the pen and I flip to a clean page and get ready for whatever she needs to dictate.

She leans back in the armchair, folds her hands over her tummy, and closes her eyes. She looks so innocent, like a real grandmother. The illusion lasts exactly until her lips move. Granny speaks slowly, as if she is considering every word, as if she is a queen writing a very important speech to her royal subjects.

"Most forests in the world consist of second-growth trees. The original forests were logged and once the old trees were gone, the original, complex forest ecosystems were destroyed. Does that make sense?"

I nod. I just want to be finished so I can get back to writing my article.

"What do you think it means?"

Before I answer I pull my lower lip between my front teeth so I don't say anything too rude. How dumb does she think I am?

"I guess the old forests and new forests are different— but you don't really say why."

Granny nods and closes her eyes again. It's so long before she speaks again I wonder if she's dozed off and how mad she'd be if I crept out of the room.

"Second-growth forests are monocultures—the trees are all the same variety, the same age, the same shape and size. In a forest that grows naturally, many more species exist together. Young trees grow over hundreds of years to replace the ancient ones when they die. When trees fall, they eventually rot and enrich the soil, ensuring a healthy start for seedlings and other forest plants."

Granny pauses but keeps her eyes shut.

"You don't really say why new forests aren't any good."

"Without the biodiversity of many types of plants and tree varieties, whole forests can be decimated by the introduction of a disease or parasite. What's wrong? Why are you laughing?"

"I've never heard of trees getting sick."

"Well, they do. Pine beetles, for example. If you have a natural, old-growth, mixed forest, some trees may get sick, but other varieties will survive and grow stronger when more nutrients, or light, or water is available after the sick trees die."

This does make some sense but I hardly have time to let it sink in before Granny is dictating the next point.

"Traditional uses of the many varieties of plants found in old-growth forests include food, medicine, ceremonial rites, dyes, and building materials. Destroying the few remaining pockets of our ancient forests like the Tarragon Woods means we destroy centuries of knowledge that will be lost forever."

"Don't you think that's a bit melodramatic?"

Granny's eyes fly open.

"I mean, the trees do grow back . . . eventually."

"You show me a logging company willing to wait eight hundred or a thousand or two thousand years for a forest to re-establish itself and I'll show you a chicken with lips!"

"I do know what you mean. I guess if some kind of mushroom or whatever dies when the trees disappear it might never come back."

"Exactly!" Granny leans forward in her chair and taps the back of my hand. "Exactly!"

Just then the phone rings.

"Granny?" Matt calls from the kitchen. "It's for you!"

"Thank you, Heather. We can do more later," she says as she lifts herself out of the armchair.

"Fine. Call me later, I guess. When you're ready."

Back in my room I look up the word EXTINCT. There are several definitions, all of them depressing. A species that has died out, a volcano that no longer erupts, life or hope that has been terminated or quenched. I think of Grandpa and how final and how sad extinction really is.

The half-written article for the paper lies like a tiger trap on the desk in front of me. I can see that it might not be good to kill off species. Who knows when some mushroom might hold the secret to the cure for cancer or zits? But I cannot believe that a bunch of tree-hugging grandmothers wearing only knitted caps and pounding bongo drums are the way to be taken seriously by the people who make the laws or decide how to harvest trees.

Nobody else interrupts until it's time for dinner. Even so, the words don't come easily and after I've finished a second brownie for dessert, I bundle up and relocate to Dove Cottage, hoping that I might have better luck outside.

I don't consider myself to be a mean person. Sure, I have moments when I don't feel like reading to Matt and I make it sound like if I don't study for a math quiz I'm going to lose my chance to attend the university of my choice. Matt gets over it. He knows I have a life. Sure, for a while he goes around looking as though his favourite hamster died . . . Okay, maybe I can be a little bit mean, but really, isn't everybody a teeny bit mean sometimes?

The rain drums the roof of Dove Cottage, louder and softer as gusts of wind drive through the storm, push it around, stir it up. Being nice has no place in journalism. It's not like fiction, the serious kind of writing I prefer where you can take charge of the story you tell. The job of the press is to relate the facts and provide balanced coverage—it's quite different. I do it for the challenge, not because it requires a whole lot of creativity. A newspaper article is not the kind of thing I'd waste time on at the writing group.

I read the piece over again. I have reported the facts. I have described things clearly. So, why do I feel as though the article I've written is mean?

But it's too late now. I promised Mr. Turnbull that I

would fax the story to the newspaper before the end of the weekend. It's nearly midnight now, and I have a lot to do tomorrow. The darkness inhales me when I blow out the candle, and I shiver. When did it get so cold? The article is stiff and prickly under my sweater. I wait a few minutes just inside the door, let my eyes adjust to the blackness, and hope the rain might ease up, even a little.

The downpour is relentless, louder than my heartbeat. Louder than my breathing. Louder than my conscience.

I clutch my arms around my stomach so the papers don't slip out and drop into a puddle. Then I run out into the rain and sprint for the warmth of the sleeping house.

Once inside, I sneak into the office and dial the fax number at the newspaper. All the while that I'm dialing, waiting for the pages to feed into the machine, listening to the strange electronic chattering as the fax machines talk to each other, my heart pounds and a frog that has mysteriously set up residence inside me does the splits, then jumping jacks, and finally curls up in a leaden ball lodged right between my ribs in the very spot on my chest that I think would kill someone if you happened to land a solid punch right there. It takes quite a while to recover after the last *beeeeep* tells me the story has gone.

Lying in bed, I can't sleep for the longest time. Every shadow holds an accusation and what I want to do is go back into the office and somehow retrieve the fax I've sent. I know that's impossible, but deep in the shadowy pit of my gut, the ache of guilt is unmistakable.

15

As a writer I'm merely a journalist who has learned to write better than others. – Gabriel García Márquez

DO NOT DISTURB

The red paint is thick and gooey and smears when I paint the letters on a piece of scrap wood, wet and slippery from the West Coast winter. Even though it looks as if someone has bled all over the sign, it's still legible enough to keep people from bothering me.

Smells of the former inhabitants of Dove Cottage rise from the damp dirt floor. The souls of dead chickens scratch around looking for worms, or whatever it is that chickens eat.

For about the millionth time I wish I had a wood stove in here. The candle barely lights because the wick is soggy. But I persevere until a flame swells; even during the day the glow seems to brighten things up. Everything on this whole entire island is soggy. I have two welcome mats, one inside and one outside the door, but even so, the old rug Granny and I threw over the hard-packed dirt is beyond grubby. In the summer I took off my shoes at the door, but now it's way too cold for that. I have three pairs of socks on and my toes are still numb.

The funny thing is, it's not as cold temperature-wise as it used to get during the winter in Ontario. But it feels cold, maybe because everything is wet. Or maybe I just notice the cold more because I spend so much time sitting around in it. In Ontario it would never have occurred to me to sit in an unheated writer's cottage in January.

Tugging the tattered quilt up around my shoulders, I curl into the beanbag, yawn, and check my watch. Five minutes to eleven.

I squirm deeper into the nest I've formed and make a bit of a tent so my pen has room to move. My breath hangs in a moist cloud in front of me when I exhale. Four minutes to go.

What image will Maggie send? What if I don't receive anything? Not that I really believe in this stuff, but Maggie and I were so close that half the time we knew what the other was going to say before she opened her mouth to speak. And who knows? Strange things happen in the world. Inexplicable things, like when Grandpa came to me in a dream and told me that if I slowed down I would notice valuable things. The very next day I was thinking about that dream and walking really slowly up the front steps to school and noticed a twenty-dollar bill fluttering in the bushes beside the building.

Even though I'm trying to stay still and quiet, a jumble of images flash through my mind: Maggie and her cat; Maggie choosing a new backpack during our last trip to our favourite shopping mall; Maggie at her writing desk;

Maggie at the writing club, laughing so hard she sprayed cookie crumbs all over the open dictionary. None of those images could be the one she's sending because in all of them, I'm there somewhere, inside the pictures. They are memories. Shared memories.

I close my eyes and try to concentrate except I don't know how to concentrate on nothing. Being curled up in a quilt is making me really sleepy—my body isn't too happy about my late night. If Maggie is going to send an image I'm actually going to be able to see, I need some kind of plain background. So, I imagine a white wall, an adobe wall like you'd find in Mexico. But then I start thinking of cactuses and sombreros and, for some reason, guns and gunfighters and no matter what I do I can't seem to turn the pictures off. A gunfight is enthralling, especially when it happens in slow motion inside my head right up to the poof of dust when one of the banditos falls to the ground.

The chances of Mags sending me a lousy Western movie isn't too likely, so I try to concentrate on Maggie's message. What is it? What do I see?

11:10 a.m. About the only thing I can think about is how stiff, cold, and weary I am. No matter how I shift and wiggle and scrunch down into the quilt, there is no way to get comfortable. So far, I haven't *seen* any kind of message from Maggie. I try something different.

Loosely gripping my pen, I lightly circle over the page and wait for some profound word to spill out.

DINOSAUR

LIGHT
BLANKET
SANDWICH

The writing is wiggly, uncertain, and ridiculous. Watching what my hand is writing, apparently without my help, is at least more interesting than freezing to death.

CHICKENS

Stupid. That's just the smell of Dove Cottage. The production of these few words has taken nearly ten minutes, each letter slowly scratched out onto the page, one wobbly letter at a time.

Another smell tickles my nostrils. Fresh baking. I breathe a little deeper and try to identify what treat awaits me once I get back into the house. Sweet, definitely something sweet. But no chocolate. I inhale deeply, drawing in a faint whiff of something lovely. Cinnamon?

I breathe in again but the smell has faded away to almost nothing. I read somewhere that sensory nerve receptors can only fire so many times in a row. Then they get tired and you can't smell any more, even when the scent still lingers in the air. I guess maybe that's why people who work in stinky places get used to the odours and don't get bothered after a while. I sniff, but either the breeze has blown the baking smells in the other direction or my nose nerves are exhausted.

I take three deep breaths to force myself to relax, but

this just makes me feel light-headed and then my hand shakes as if it really wants to write something so I let it go and it spews this:

Writer Girl glares at her spasmed hand as if it were an alien life force attached to the end of her arm, clamped around her pen. "Be free to write words of wisdom from the other side—"

Creepy. I move my pen in slow circles across the page, kind of like when we learned the cursive letter *e* in grade two except back then my work was neater. SPASMED. I don't think that's even a real word. *Hopeless,* I write.

Heather, you are useless as a psychic. Cat. Hat. Mat.

Scrunching my eyes shut as tightly as I can, I exhale, trying to send all the stupid, noisy thoughts out with my breath.

PONYTAIL
HAIR CLIPS
HAIRBRUSH
FOOTSTOOL
CARPET
WORMS
MR. SAUNDERSON
SLEIGH BELLS

Words spew out of my pen faster than I can write,

getting messier and messier as they sprawl across the page.

BRIDE
SLIPPERY
TOW TRUCK
CHOCOLATE COINS WRAPPED IN GOLD FOIL

It's kind of exciting.

CANDY NECKLACE
JAM
FLEAS

I get to the bottom of the page, flip it over, and keep scribbling.

CANOE RACE
RED-BEARD PIRATE
THOSE FISH THAT EAT PEOPLE

I scratch out a picture of a teepee and some arrows pointing to the word LOCKED and then draw a big circle around the word AMBULANCE at which point I shudder and my pen stops splattering words all over the page.

Inside my head, thoughts keep going.

Writer Girl lifts her hand, examines it for . . . for claw marks, as if some beast has released her wrist. Sadness engulfs her for she knows that without the help of the monster she will never write again.

11:20.

What on earth was Maggie thinking about? Canoe race? Hairbrush?

I'm tempted to go straight inside and make some hot chocolate to go with whatever treats Matt is whipping up. I obviously didn't receive anything from Maggie, and I could become seriously hypothermic by staying out here to send her a message that probably won't go anywhere. Ontario is such a long way away.

By 11:29 a wave of guilt persuades me to relocate to my writing desk, the quilt pulled right up over my head. So I don't confuse Maggie the way she confused me, I have placed just two objects in front of me that I brought outside from my bedroom. Maybe Maggie's psychic tuning receiver works better than mine.

At exactly 11:30 I pick up a card that Maggie made for me back when I lived in Ontario. I hold it between my hands, flat, as though I'm making pancakes from clay. I stroke it front and back and then study the drawing on the front. Two little girls with triangle dresses and figure-eight bows in their hair play outside a house. Maggie's colouring was always better than mine, and now, as I examine every single detail, I trace over one of the bows with my fingertip, then slow down and go over it again with my mind.

I read the words inside over and over, first to myself and then aloud, though softly, in case anyone happens to walk past outside.

Your very best friend for ever and ever.

Though it feels as if this huge effort of concentration takes two hours, when I check my watch, it's only three minutes into my designated sending time. Wow. If Maggie worked this hard at her end, I wonder if she lasted the whole half-hour? I could hardly blame her if she gave up after a short while. This psychic stuff is hard work!

I switch to the other object—a starfish about the size of a dollar coin that I found on the beach the other day. Again, I inspect every last bump, groove, and shade of colour, top and bottom, of each of the creature's five legs.

I do this three times until it feels as though the starfish has invaded every available neuron in my brain.

Then, my stomach rumbles and I realize the delicious smell is back, stronger this time. I turn my head toward the door, half expecting Matt or Granny to be standing there with a tray full of cookies fresh from the oven. Nobody's there and when I breathe in again, the smell has faded away.

11:45. I look back over at the card but I can't imagine how I could possibly send a picture that was any clearer than the one I did. Besides, if I don't move, I am in serious danger of dying out here and then I'd have to haunt Maggie from beyond the grave to communicate with her.

As slowly as I can, I make my way back to the house. In one hand I hold the card and in the other the starfish. Each step I take I say one or the other under my breath: CARD, STARFISH, CARD, STARFISH. Even though I take baby steps, I reach the back steps long before noon. Oh well, that will have to do. I'm starving.

"It's hot in here!" I can't get out of my hat and woolly scarf fast enough.

"It's you," Matt and Granny say together.

"Can I have one?" I ask, reaching for a big plate of muffins.

"May I?" Matt and Granny say, again in unison.

"You guys are like evil twins."

Granny chuckles. "Evil. That's us. Help yourself, but watch out for the poisoned ones!"

"Ha ha."

The muffin is superb—banana and some kind of nut. "Walnuts?"

"Pecans," they say together.

We all laugh and then, as if scripted for a dumb movie, they do the silent jinx by pretending to zip their lips shut, turn twin invisible keys, and toss them over their shoulders. I wonder who will speak first, and if Matt can survive a good tickling. The door slams open again.

"Ready to go?" Dad asks.

Granny looks at her watch, then at Matt, then at me before she pretends to retrieve her invisible key to unlock her jinxed lips.

"Already? Are you coming with us, Heather?"

"Back to the blockade?"

"I'm coming!" Matt shouts.

"Warm boots. Heavy jacket," Granny says. "Yes,

Heather, of course you can come, too."

The frog from last night returns suddenly, rolling over inside my stomach and forcing me to put down my muffin. After what I wrote for the paper it probably isn't the best idea to be seen on the logging road.

"I think I'll stay here. I've got homework."

Granny nods. "If you have time, maybe you could work on the information sheets. Look up the Tarragon Woods website and add some stuff about the watershed and the owls, the endangered ones that only nest—"

"In old-growth forests."

Granny grins at me, her soft cheeks folding around deep dimples.

"Good girl!"

The frog in my stomach kicks both bulgy back legs into my gut. If only Granny knew how *not* good I am.

I manage a weak smile and take my muffin up to my room. I force it down, imagining each mouthful is a lump of concrete crashing down on the frog's head.

Feeling totally ill and mad at myself for not grabbing something to drink, I have to risk a quick trip to the kitchen. I reach for the tap just as Dad sticks his head in through the door and snatches up our big umbrella.

"What are you going to work on?"

"My socials project. The one about the Middle Ages."

I'm actually enjoying this unit because I talked my teacher into letting me write a journal as if I were a peasant girl living near a castle way back in the 1300s. (Why is it that the 1300s are also known as the 14th century? How confusing is that?) Anyway, it's turning out to be a huge amount of work and it's due by the end of the week.

I'm not just writing the assignment by hand instead of on the computer. I'm also soaking paper in tea, burning the edges, and then adding fancy painted letters at the beginning of each page. It looks just like those illuminated manuscripts you see in books. Dad let me use some of this gold paint he has and the part that I've finished looks pretty good.

"Don't do any more burning while we're gone," Dad says, "unless your mother comes back."

"I know. I won't."

"We should be back before dinner. We'll bring something in from town—pizza maybe."

"No broccoli on mine." I'm still not used to the odd mix of pizza toppings you get on this island. Pesto. Refried beans. Broccoli. What are these people thinking? What's wrong with pepperoni and mushrooms? Though I'm never sure if I should trust the mushrooms they use around here. I've heard stories that people collect funny mushrooms that make you hallucinate if you eat enough of them. Unless they kill you, that is. Two people last year wound up in the emergency room of the hospital because they accidentally ate these really poisonous mushrooms they picked at the north end of the island. Personally, I'm terrified of any mushroom that doesn't come out of a can.

The door shuts and I think I'm safe, but almost right away Dad pokes his head back inside.

"Heather?"

"What?"

"Can you feed the dog?"

Mia looks up at me and wags her tail. She's pretty smart. She knows her name is Mia, That Animal, or The Dog, according to whether she's been good, bad, or neutral.

I nod. "Why aren't you taking her?"

Granny huffs into the kitchen carrying a huge backpack. Two cooking pots hanging from the back clank together when she plunks it on the kitchen floor. "Rule change. It's too hard to keep track of dogs out there. And there were some problems when owners got arrested and they couldn't take their dogs to jail."

"I thought you were already out in the truck! Where's Matt?"

"In the truck," Dad says, handing Granny the umbrella.

"How long are you planning to stay out there this time?"

"As long as it takes, Heather."

"What if you get arrested again?"

"I'm not planning to get arrested. I really don't think the police were too happy about arresting anybody last time. The government is going to have to find a better way to deal with this situation."

She sounds so reasonable, so determined. The frog kicks again.

"We've got to go. The photographer will be there in forty-five minutes." Granny winks at me. "We're taking some publicity shots today—for the website."

I don't even ask whether the grannies are planning to

wear more than hats and mittens. I do not wish to know the sordid details. When Granny holds the door open for Dad, who has picked up Granny's pack, a gust of wind blows a few soggy leaves into the kitchen. It's pouring again and I hope this is enough to discourage any foolish disrobing in the forest. A bunch of old ladies with pneumonia won't be much use to anyone.

"Be careful," I say as the door closes behind them, but I don't think they hear me.

Before I can possibly settle down to my homework, I make myself a cup of hot chocolate and scrounge around for some cookies to supplement the muffin. Unfortunately, all that the campers have left me is a box of stale crackers. Every last crumb of Matt's tasty baking has gone to the front lines to feed the wrinkle brigade.

Back in my room, my gaze falls on Maggie's card propped up against my reading lamp. Maggie. I could call her, see what she has to say about our experiment.

I dial her number, but at the other end of the line the phone rings and rings and rings. With each ring the longing for Maggie's voice gets stronger until I don't care at all whether she sent or received anything. I just want to talk to her, to laugh at a stupid knock-knock joke, hear how her cat is doing. I will her to pick up the phone, to say "Howdy" in her inimitable Maggie way. *Ring. Ring. Ring.* When the answering machine finally picks up I am so close to tears I don't trust myself to speak. Instead, I hang up before the beep.

16

Writing is not necessarily something to be ashamed of, but do it in private and wash your hands afterwards.

— Robert A. Heinlein

The first comments about the article find me at lunch-time on Wednesday. They don't come from the places I might have expected, like teachers or kids in the writing group. The first guy to comment is Rob Cardinal, a cap kid and one of Jerry Bastion's friends.

Rob doesn't actually say anything. He flips both thumbs up at me and gives me a slow nod in the hallway. Two of his friends, also wearing ball caps emblazoned with logging company logos, bob their heads. It might not sound like much, but these kids are big and tough and they belong to what Granny considers to be the enemy camp. If I had placed a bet on who had painted my locker, I would have guessed Rob and his buddies or any of the others who have taken the side of the loggers.

Our school is not the only place dividing into two groups: so is the rest of the town. There are plenty of people on this island whom Dad calls "Greenies." They're the people who sell their organic squash at the market, or wear hemp shirts and hand-braided friendship bracelets dyed with crushed-up flower petals, or who live in energy-efficient underground houses like our neighbours, the Cranwells.

Lots of the shop windows have posters and signs up that declare "SAVE THE TARRAGON WOODS! NO MORE LOGGING!" or "TREES ARE THE LUNGS OF OUR PLANET" or "PRESERVE OUR PRECIOUS FORESTS FOR FUTURE GENERATIONS."

I guess I'm part of the future generations they're talking about, but I also have to agree with the signs put up by the other side.

They say things like "LOGGERS NEED LOVE TOO" and "HARVEST TREES WITH CARE AND FUTURE FORESTS WILL TAKE CARE OF YOU" and "WHAT'S THAT WOODEN CHAIR YOU'RE SITTING ON?" That last sign is hanging up in the Egg-zachly Coffee Shop opposite the gas station. I was a bit surprised to see it, actually, because the owner, Zach, looks like one of the Greenies, what with his long ponytail and shell necklace, but Dad says he's the son of a logger and that his family owns a huge woodlot at the north end of the island.

To be fair, there's also a sign up in the window that says, "LOVE YOUR TREES, LOVE YOUR FUTURE." I guess that's maybe to keep the Greenies coming back for regular doses of herbal tea and pumpkin seed cookies.

When I get home from school, nobody greets me with

a thumbs-up. Instead, the minute he sees me, Dad leaves the kitchen and disappears into his studio. Matt sticks his tongue out at me. Granny is nowhere to be seen, though I'm pretty sure Dad said she was coming home today, and Mom is still busy in the clinic. The newspaper lies open on the kitchen table, my article huge and ugly on the page.

Responsible Citizens or Lowly Criminals?
Life in the War Zone
By Heather Blake

They say all is fair in love and war and some citizens who love trees take this idea very seriously. These soldiers in the battle to protect trees insist they have the right to protest on public property. I guess I don't have a problem with that except I think they forget about the other part of being a good citizen, and that's being responsible. It's like when my family goes out for a picnic in a public park—we always make sure we are responsible and pick up our garbage and don't trample on flowers. So these warriors should remember their responsibilities to their friends, family, and fellow taxpayers.

If protesters like the Ladies of the Forest decide to march around with flags or signs saying they don't like people cutting down trees, that's okay. That's what it means to live in a democracy. But is it acceptable for them to stop people from going to work? What happens to the people who make a living in the forest? How are they supposed to feed their children when they can't drive along a public road to get to their jobs? Public roads belong to loggers, too.

Another thing that the Ladies of the Forest don't think about is what will happen to the people in their families when they do embarrassing and illegal things. It can cost a lot to hire a lawyer to get a relative out of jail and being a criminal can affect the kinds of jobs protesters can get. Is it responsible to become a criminal by choice? What would happen to me, for example, if my grandmother was in jail and my parents were killed in an accident? Would the government put me in an orphanage? Who would pay to take care of me? And, at the same time, who has to pay the bills to keep my grandmother locked up in jail when the jail space should be used for really bad people? (My grandmother is not a bad person, even though she is doing some things that are wrong, in my opinion.)

If protesters are really worried about the forest, they should write letters to the government, vote for different people in the next election, and maybe have meetings with the logging companies to see about making more parks.

And, finally, I don't think a lot of people really want to see older females without their clothes on—I know I don't like it and lots of little kids could see these inappropriate photographs in stores and homes in our community.

I don't know why I read it again—I already know what I said. But it's like when I have a scab and I pick at it, just to make sure things are healing properly, and

I wind up making everything bleed again. By the time I get to the part about Granny going to jail, my parents dying, and me going to an orphanage, I figure nobody in my family will ever speak to me again. Not only that, I could probably pick any one of the cap kids if I needed a date to take to a school dance. Who would have ever dreamed that would be true?

We can't ignore each other at dinner, though we all try. Unfortunately, Mom and Dad have always had this theory that it's important to sit down together once a day to share a meal, even if it's a quick meal and nobody has a whole lot of time to chat.

It would almost be easier if they all yelled at me, or sent me to my room, but Mom studies a veterinary supply catalogue as if her life depends on getting a great deal on cotton swabs, and Dad cuts his green beans up into tiny sections that he pushes around his plate before stabbing them with his fork. Granny appears at the table and silently scoops a serving of lasagna onto her plate. She sits beside Matt, leaving the chair beside me empty. Once, when she thinks I'm not looking, Granny reaches over and squeezes Matt's hand.

Of course I know why they're all mad, but I don't think I have anything to apologize about, so I don't say anything. When I do speak, it's to let them know I'm leaving. "I'll be out in Dove Cottage," I tell them as soon as I've wolfed down a piece of apple pie. Nobody tries to stop me, not even Mom, who would usually tell me I can't go anywhere until the dishes are washed.

"Come on, Mia." I pat my leg and Mia scrambles out

from under the table. I don't look back, but as I head out the kitchen door, I feel four sets of eyeballs glaring at my back.

I haven't been out at my desk for more than three minutes before there's a soft knock at the door.

"Heather?"

I fling my pen down. Why does Mom need to bother me out here? Why couldn't she talk to me in the house?

"What?"

She doesn't scold me for my less-than-welcoming tone, but pushes the wooden door open and ducks inside.

"Heather, we have to talk."

"Why?"

Mom looks up into a dusty corner and sighs. "Nice cobwebs." She pulls up a wooden crate and eases herself down, wary when the old thing creaks. "Your grandmother is quite upset."

I don't say anything. I can tell Mom is gearing up for a lecture.

"Oh, Heather. What were you thinking?"

I bite my bottom lip hard, determined not to cry.

Instead of yelling at me, Mom reaches over and pats my leg. This just makes things worse and I am horrified to hear a sniffle followed by a shuddery breath. I clamp my mouth shut and breathe loudly through my nose.

"Heather, there are plenty of people who agree with you about a lot of the things you said in the article."

"A journalist has to be fair," I say, but my voice is all wobbly, so it doesn't really sound too convincing.

"Yes, I agree. But Heather, were you really fair? Did

you interview your grandmother? How well do you understand Granny's side of the story?"

Does she understand *my* side of the story? Mom waits for me to answer. I roll my pen back and forth between my palms. Back and forth. Back and forth.

"Can you stop doing that?"

A breeze outside swishes the leafless bramble stalks against the back of Dove Cottage. They are the most persistent of plants, like something out of a science fiction movie. Blackberries will be the evil, thorny vines that eat New York.

"Heather . . ."

I look at my mother properly for the first time since she invaded my writing place, expecting to see her eyes blazing, smoke pouring from her ears. But she doesn't seem angry; her eyes and her voice are soft. "Heather, I . . . you do understand what I mean when I say my comments are 'off the record'?" I nod and she continues, "I agree with you, to a certain extent."

"You do?"

"How do you think it makes me feel to see my mother parading around like that?"

I put the pen down and see now that Mom's face is tight and pale. She's pulled her thick, unruly hair into a loose bun at the back of her neck and several strands have escaped. It strikes me that she looks as though she's coming undone, and I feel a small knot of fear in my stomach. More than anything I want to go to her, to put my arms around her and comfort her, but my hands stay still, folded in my lap.

"And I have a business to run. This is a very small community."

She doesn't need to tell me! Not a day passes that I don't think about how small this place is.

"So why don't you stop her?"

"Oh, Heather—don't cry. I know this is hard for you."

All hope of warding off tears disappears when Mom reaches out to hug me and I dissolve in misery. Mom rubs my back and makes the same noises she uses when she's tending to an injured animal.

"I can't stop her. Your grandmother is a grown woman. A woman with a mission. I may not agree with her tactics, but I have to respect her convictions, her choices."

"But she doesn't . . . she doesn't . . ." It takes me a minute to pull myself together enough to continue. "But Granny doesn't respect *us*—otherwise why would she put us through this?" Images of Jerry Bastion and his friends and the spray paint on my locker push into my head and I nearly start sobbing again. "You don't know what it's like at school."

"Oh, Heather. I do know what's happening. Mrs. Gurney is doing the best she can." Mom rubs my back. "I am sorry about what you're going through."

It doesn't feel any better to hear my mother apologizing. She isn't the one causing all the problems.

"But just because you don't agree with someone doesn't mean you have the right to write a one-sided article. You have a gift, Heather. And you also have a responsibility—to tell both sides of the story."

And that's when I really lose it. It's like a tornado is tearing apart the inside of my body. If Mom is still making those soothing little noises, I don't hear her. I make such a racket you'd think someone was chopping off my hands with a chainsaw.

When I finally regain my senses and become aware of Mom's arms around me, her hand stroking my hair, a terrible thought comes to me. Through sniffles and hiccupping noises I ask, "Do I . . . do I ha-ha-ave to write another story?"

"Oh, Heather. I can't tell you what to do." At that moment I wish she would, but all she says is, "Shhhhh, now. You don't have to make any decisions right now. Why don't you come into the house and I'll bring you a cup of hot chocolate in your room."

"Tell them I . . . I don't w-want to see anybody."

Mom nods. "I'll pass the message along." Her dark brown eyes warm with her smile. It's only then that I realize that Mia's chin is on my foot. When I reach down to stroke her silky ears a slow wiggle travels down the length of her slightly pudgy body and ends with a wave of her tail.

Mia follows me inside and upstairs and then scrambles up onto my bed and rests her head on her paws. Under her twitchy eyebrows, her eyes follow my every move. Somehow, having Mia with me makes me feel a little better. I lie on the bed beside her, rubbing the special spot behind her ear until her back leg starts thumping and I smile. My moment of feeling a teeny bit better doesn't last long. When the hot chocolate arrives, Granny is the one who gently places it on my nightstand and then sits beside me on the bed.

"Do you have any idea how many letters I've written?" Granny says, reaching to scratch Mia's tummy. Mia squiggles onto her back, licks her lips, and sighs.

"Letters?"

"To government people. To the forestry companies. To the media people. Ben's Boards and Buckets. What good did it do? The trucks kept rolling up the logging road."

"Ben's? Why did you write to the hardware store?"

"I was trying to get them to buy only locally milled wood—and to encourage them to buy locally made wood furniture."

This sounds completely crazy to me. "I thought you didn't want people to use trees!"

"What I don't want is for people to waste the few ancient trees we have left. I don't want any more clear-cutting, where all the trees are chopped down at the same time. It's cheap to cut trees like that, but Heather, the damage!"

"I still don't get why you're encouraging Ben's to buy wood furniture or local boards or whatever. What about plastic?"

Granny sighs and looks at the ceiling as if she's hoping to find inspiration up there.

"Furniture can be made from second-growth trees. Say a forest worker takes one tree down—he can sell that tree to a factory in another province or even another country and somebody else can make it into a table and get far more money from that table than the cost of the log.

"If the same tree stays in town and goes to a local craftsperson—a furniture maker—maybe it would take a week for them to make a table. The money they earn doing that might buy groceries or pay a local person to patch a hole in their roof. So, a community could keep more of the money earned by carefully harvesting trees and developing industries locally, or—"

"Okay. I understand all that."

"I don't think you understand how important it is—"

"I do." I say it so loudly that Granny leans back, almost as though I pushed her. "I understand about biodiversity and how clear-cutting causes erosion and landslides, how mud washing into creeks wrecks the places where salmon lay eggs." I talk faster and faster, my cheeks burning, and I watch my grandmother's expression change from patient teacher to someone who is completely confused. And I love this feeling of confusing her because maybe now she knows just a tiny bit of how I feel when she acts like such a crazy person.

"They teach us all this stuff in school—about ecosystems, and habitats, and how trees are like the lungs of the planet."

"Heather, if you know all this, then how could you write that article?"

"Because none of that is the point!" At which point a really horrible noise—part growl, part groan, part sob, part strangled screech tries very hard to escape my throat and I throw myself sideways and bury my head in the pillow.

"Oh, Heather," Granny says, patting my back.

The noise comes out again, except more muffled and somewhat soggy. I burrow harder into the pillow. How can I have so little self-control? What kind of an immature baby am I?

"Shhh . . . that's it, cry it out."

Her words make me want to stuff my whole pillow down my throat so no more disgusting, weak, furious noises come out, but even this thought of trying to stop makes me cry harder and I just give in to what must surely be the life of abject misery I am doomed to live.

Whatever the loggers are doing hurts only a bunch of trees. I don't care about protecting my so-called future, tree-filled or not. What my grandmother is doing is hurting me *now*. And the way she coos and hushes makes it all worse because I know she does love me. She just doesn't care enough to restrain herself, stop fighting, and find some other way to make her point.

17

The test of any good fiction is that you should care
something for the characters; the good to succeed, the
bad to fail. The trouble with most fiction is that you want
them all to land in hell, together, as quickly as possible.

—Mark Twain

"I think what she did was cool—and not like her at all."
Eric's voice is loud, sure of himself.

Are they talking about me? I stop just outside the
room, not really wanting to know but not able to make
my hand reach out to push open the door.

Willow's slow drawl doesn't change when she says, "I
think what she did was cowardly. Stupid. Just like her.
Who does she think she is? Those women are heroes.
Heroines. Heras."

"Willow! That's not fair. Heather's the one who
started that Kids Saving the World group, or whatever
it's called."

"I heard it wasn't really her—it was that other girl,
Melissa . . . Alyssa . . . Alyssum or whatever she's called.
Heather probably went along with it because she thought

it would make people like her."

My face is so hot I feel like I've got a fever. I unzip my jacket, still unable to move.

"She must have had a reason for writing the article the way she did." It takes a moment for me to place the voice. Karin. The new girl. The filmmaker.

There's no way I can stay for tonight's meeting. How can I defend myself? Why do I feel I have to defend myself? I turn around and reach for the door to go back outside. My fingers brush the knob and I let out a shriek as the door is yanked from my hand and Custer crashes into me.

"Hey!" he says. "Isn't the group meeting tonight?"

"Yeah, it is. I just got here. I was trying to . . . catch my dad. He drove off with my, with . . . with something in the car. It doesn't matter. He's gone."

Custer pulls the door shut with a bang and we walk into the meeting room together and are met with a round of hellos. Karin moves to the middle of the couch and pats the space on either side of her. "Hi, guys."

"I guess that's everybody," Eric says. I try to catch his eye but there's no reassuring wink, no stupid grin. He's all business. "Shall we get started?"

Eric talks about a problem he's having with his new mystery novel. "If I could figure out why Jason wants to help find the murderer, that would make the whole story more believable." He reads a scene where the murderer is hiding a body in a used car lot. It's really creepy, partly because Eric only ever describes the murderer's hands—wrapped around a crowbar he uses to pry open locked trunks. The scariest part is when Eric reads about the murderer's fingers unwrapping a piece of gum and you realize those hands could belong to anyone.

Custer is next. He pulls several notebooks from his bag and flips through pages, showing us panels from three different storylines.

"Wow. You've been busy," Karin says.

"Doodling," Wynd adds.

Custer ignores Wynd and we move closer so we can see the pictures and read over his shoulder. The part I like best is where he shows a child being run over by an ice cream truck. Not that I'm overly morbid, but the way he has drawn the sequence of panels it's as though the scene happens in slow motion and is viewed from several camera angles. Custer has shown the driver's contorted mouth, the view from inside the cab, looking down on the girl's startled face, what the girl sees as the truck bears down on her (a distorted grille and giant cut-out of an ice cream cone). The only words are some sound effects—the squeal of brakes, a dull thud, the musical notes of the truck continuing to play the ice cream song as a crowd gathers. The dialogue is minimal (the truck driver swears just before impact).

How many pages of writing would it take for me to describe all of that? None of us have much in the way of suggestions. Everyone, even Wynd, seems to like his story so far.

"What are you working on?" Eric asks Wynd.

One side of Wynd's lip twists upward and she plunks a fat file folder on the table. Inside are pages and pages of her loopy handwriting interspersed with photo collages of faces cut from magazines. She has altered the faces with paint or something so they all look like they have been dug up from the grave. Wynd always seems to be trying to scare people, make them think she is deeply disturbed.

"I'm experimenting with writing a story using different narrators," I say when it's my turn. "I don't have one main character. I think the final story will have four main people in it—sort of four stories in one."

"Any of your characters loggers? Protesters?" Willow asks, her face the picture of innocence, her voice sweet, curious.

"Hey—you're the one who wrote that article, right?" Custer asks, leaning forward. He laughs and adds, "I just figured that out."

I sigh. I should have pushed right past him, into the cold, and sat somewhere out of the wind until it was time to go home. Anything would have been better than dealing with this.

Custer barges right on, completely oblivious to my discomfort. "I thought it was great. My dad cut it out and stuck it on the fridge."

It's a very creepy thought that the words I wrote in the privacy of Dove Cottage are now displayed on someone's fridge. Custer's fridge, no less.

"Your dad's probably a logger, right?" Willow asks.

"Well, he doesn't work out in the woods. He's in the office at BIFI. He's an accountant."

"Can we not talk about this?" I say.

"Why not, Heather?" Wynd asks. "Are you feeling bad because you said uncharitable things about your dear, naked grandmother?"

Nobody is rude enough to laugh out loud, but Eric blushes and disappears right under the coffee table, ostensibly searching for his pen.

"Hey—what those women are doing is amazing," Karin says. "How does your grandmother feel about the article?"

Any gratitude I might have felt toward Karin for sticking up for me dissipates when she turns to me and picks up her pen, ready to scribble down my answer.

"I don't know. I try not to talk to my grandmother much these days." Thinking about our horrible conversation in my bedroom brings a lump to my throat.

Eric makes a strange noise under the table, as if he's swallowed something spicy. He bumps his head as he manoeuvres out of his hiding place and tries to regain control of the meeting.

"Are you going to read something?"

I shake my head, uncertain how my voice might sound.

"Sure?"

I nod and Eric turns to Karin. "What have you got?"

"I was out filming on the front lines. Got some great stuff. I brought a videotape. Does that thing work?" She points at an ancient television set beside the bricked-in fireplace.

Eric shrugs. "Let's give it a try."

My silent prayers that the decrepit VCR might not

function are ignored. It takes only a minute for Karin to get her tape into the machine, and an image of a giant tree appears on the screen. "This is still really rough," she says. "I still have lots of editing to do."

"How do you edit?" Eric asks.

"On my computer. Everything is digital, even the music. Then I copy finished scenes that I like onto tape so I can show my stuff more easily. Oh, here's what I want you to see. I was thinking of making this the beginning of the film."

The camera slowly moves up the trunk of the tree. A flute plays a simple, haunting melody, the kind of thing you might hear in a disaster movie, just before something really gross happens. An eagle cries and then, way off in the distance, the sound of African drums fades in. By this point, the camera has reached the top of the tree and starts to turn.

"Oh, man. I'm getting seasick," Wynd groans.

I find myself swaying and catch myself because I'm also feeling a bit queasy.

"This is too long," Willow says. "You don't want people puking in the theatre."

"That's disgusting!" Custer says and then quickly adds, "The puking, I mean."

Karin writes something in her notebook. Then, the screen goes black and we hear an old woman's voice. "These trees belong to my grandchildren. These old beauties are a legacy for the future."

The drums get louder and now we can also hear women chanting, "We are stronger than before . . ." The screen is still black.

"Isn't this cheating?" Wynd asks. "Having all this blackness?"

"It's supposed to make you focus on the voice, what the woman is saying," Eric says. Who died and made him an expert on making movies? Karin gives him a little smile and makes another note.

"If we don't fight for these trees, who will?" This voice isn't quite as rickety as the first one, but the speaker has a strong foreign accent. "In my country, we cut down all of our trees hundreds of years ago. It is a lie to say these great old forests will grow back again the way they are now."

Words appear on the screen that say "Forests are not farms" and I must admit it's quite a cool effect the way that Karin has the letters grow tall and thin and then makes them all fall over as if they've been blown over— or chopped down.

Another voice speaks as the camera shows a logger with a chainsaw.

"Cutting trees in our watershed threatens our water supply. You tell me who doesn't need water to survive?"

The logger pulls the starter cord and the chainsaw roars. Then, the screen breaks up into the speckled black-and-white blizzard and noisy fuzz of a blank tape.

"That's it?" Willow asks.

"It took all week to do that much. I know it's still rough. But I want your feedback."

Nobody says anything.

"It's okay. I'm tough. You can be honest. My moms

are really brutal critics. Believe me, I can handle it. Are you interested in finding out what happens next? Who these women are? Why they're saving trees?"

I wonder whether Eric also heard what I heard, that Karin has multiple mothers. He's just nodding, his eyebrows pushed together the way they are whenever he's about to launch into some long-winded critique.

"Well, what I think is that you should start with a shot of the women, rather than the trees." He seems to be deliberately avoiding looking at me, even though I'm sitting practically right in front of him. "Like have the women naked or something."

Wynd wallops Eric on the side of the head.

"That is such a guy thing to say. Can't you think about anything else?"

"Ow! I didn't say that because I want to look at a bunch of saggy old ladies." His eyes flit past me and he blushes. "I mean, that's not why I suggested—" He sighs and tries again. "If a movie is like a book, then you need to get the attention of your audience, right? So, why not use a scene where people will really pay attention?"

He looks at Karin, but all she does is scribble more notes.

Willow leans forward and she taps her pen against her chin.

"You know, at first I thought like Wynd, that Eric was being gross. But he has a point. No offence or anything, but a tree is kind of boring to look at. I liked your falling-over letters, though. They were really cool."

"And I like the voices of the women," Eric says. "And

maybe it would be more effective to first have the voices and then maybe cut to a scene where they don't have clothes on."

Karin nods and keeps scribbling. She's already filled nearly a whole page.

"What about some loggers?" Custer asks.

"Oooh, naked loggers. I like that idea," Willow says and giggles.

"No," Custer says, not amused. "Are you going to interview any loggers?"

Karin shakes her head. "I wasn't planning to. I want this to be a story about these old women who feel so strongly about the forests that they are willing to do just about anything to save them. I'm not trying to be impartial."

"Isn't a documentary supposed to be impartial?" I ask.

"Like your article?"

"There's nothing wrong with my article."

"How can you say that?" Karin pulls a copy out of her notebook and reads aloud. "Who has to pay the bills to keep my grandmother locked up in jail when the jail space should be used for really bad people . . ."

"I know what my article said. I wrote it, remember?"

"Don't you care about the trees? The environment? Our water supply?"

"Hey, Karin—"

But Karin ignores Eric and blasts right on. "You're just as bad as the logging companies!"

"Can I say something here?"

We both glare at Custer. He doesn't wait for our

approval to continue. "The logging companies care about trees. They have to care or thousands of people would be out of work. Duh. Everyone forgets that part. And protesters never talk about how many trees get planted by the companies every year."

"I care about trees! I don't know why everybody thinks I don't!" My hands are shaking so badly I drop my pen. But when I speak, my voice is loud and strong. "I have a problem with the way some people get so high and mighty about what they think is right that they forget about having some respect for the rest of the world. Those old ladies may love trees but they don't care about people!"

"That's the *stupidest* thing I have ever heard. Your grandmother is saving those trees for *you*!"

"Well, I never asked her to!"

"You see?" Karin nods triumphantly at Eric. "She doesn't give a flying shit about the trees!"

There are all kinds of ways writers describe a silence like the one that follows Karin's outburst. Thick enough to cut with a knife. Oppressive. Stunned.

To me, it feels as though I'm in some kind of sound-proof bubble, or my ears are filled with water, or I'm looking at a scene in a movie—I'm here but I'm not here. We're all held in a spell of immobility, time moving so slowly we all seem to be trapped inside one of Custer's slow-motion cartoon sequences.

"All righty, then," Eric says finally. "Who wants to go next?"

18

Never leave home without a notebook. —Evvy Ryter

"Where is everybody?" I ask after Eric's mom drops me off at home.

Mom and Dad look at each other. And then Mom says, "You'd better sit down, Heather."

"What's going on?" It is impossible to read the expression on their faces. Dad grips his coffee cup, as if he's scared it's going to leap right out of his hands and off the table. Mom licks her lips and then lays her hands on the table, palms flat, fingers spread wide.

"Mom, what's going on?"

"Your grandmother isn't coming home tonight."

This in itself doesn't seem to be particularly bad news. If Granny stays out on the blockade all night with her friends it won't be the first time. "So? What else is new?"

Mom looks at Dad and Dad looks at his coffee cup.

"You guys, what is going on?"

"Heather, it looks like there's going to be trouble.

There were a lot of police at the blockade this evening."

"So? There were a lot of police at the blockade the other day as well."

"There are more this time. Some extra officers came from off-island."

"Hey! Where's Matt?"

The skin over Dad's cheeks stretches tight.

"He's not still out there, is he?"

"Matt wanted to stay with his grandmother."

"And you let him stay? With known criminals? And the police moving in?"

"Heather! Let's not be too melodramatic. You are talking about your grandmother," Mom says.

"She doesn't care if she goes to jail."

Dad takes a deep breath. "There are plenty of people on this island who really admire your grandmother for what she's doing."

I want to say that I'm not one of them but I suspect a comment like that wouldn't be well received.

"Why aren't you there with Matt?"

A strange look passes between my parents.

"Ask your mother."

"Mom?"

"Because we only had one vehicle and I didn't want you to arrive home to an empty house." She swishes her tea around and around in her cup. Maybe Dad will let it go.

"Bobbi?"

"Ben, this is not appropriate." Swish. Swish.

"Heather is right in the middle of this debate. She deserves a proper answer." To me, he says, "I thought we should stay with Matt and Granny but your mother felt she could not stay up at the blockade."

"I can't risk getting arrested, Ben."

I think of my mother's words about her business, her place in the community, her own discomfort with her mother's strategies.

"But how could you leave Matt?"

"That's why I'm going back up there." Dad avoids looking at my mother.

"Now? In the middle of the night?"

"I'll sleep in the truck. But I should be there in case something happens."

He doesn't say it, but his accusing glare at my mother as he picks up the keys says it all. *And so should you.*

"Matt will be okay," Dad says to me as he pulls on his coat.

Mom swirls the dregs of her tea round and round the bottom of her cup.

"Stop doing that," Dad snaps.

Mom and I both look at him, shocked.

"I'll see you tomorrow," Dad says and bangs out the door.

Later, lying in the dark upstairs, I know that both my parents have lost their minds. How could responsible people leave their child in the middle of the forest with a bunch of crazy old ladies who don't care whether or not they are going to get arrested? What if there's some kind of fight? A struggle? Matt is pretty tall for his age. What if the police grab him and don't realize that he's just a kid? What if Dad is sound asleep in the truck when it happens? If I could drive, I would hustle out to the protesters' camp and rescue him, kidnap him the way they do when someone has been brainwashed by a cult.

Writer Girl races toward protesters who chant songs in the dark forest. She leaps from her bright red sports car and runs toward the old woman and her grandson just as a police officer is about to slap handcuffs on the old lady's wrists. Weeping, the boy throws himself into her arms.

"You're here just in the nick of time!"

Of course, I don't have my licence so I can't go anywhere. I'm stuck here. Stuck. Stuck. Stuck. Usually, I am able to fall asleep as soon as my head hits the pillow and I disappear into the world of dreams. But tonight there is no such easy escape. I hear Mom running water to brush her teeth, the bedroom door closing, and, finally, quiet. I wonder how Dad is doing out in the truck. He's probably cold and has a stiff neck. I can't decide whether to be mad at him for fighting with Mom or grateful because at least he seems to care what happens to Matt. Both, I guess, if that's possible.

As the house settles down to sleep, the cat pads into my room. Tony likes to sleep with Matt, but tonight he sniffs at the top of my blanket until I lift it slightly so he can crawl underneath. Tony curls into a soft rumbling ball against my tummy. I stroke him and his paws knead the mattress as we both sink into a rescuing sleep.

For several days Matt and Granny stay out at the protest camp. So do the police, though they don't seem to be arresting anyone. And that's a good thing, I suppose. Every day Mom and Dad argue about letting Matt stay with Granny. Then, one or both of them (though it's usually Dad) goes into the camp with food, blankets, clean underwear—the kind of stuff you'd expect parents to take their children, petulant children who refuse to come home. After the first uncomfortable night in the truck, Dad doesn't sleep out there, but often his first trip out to the front lines is right after he drops me off at school.

Even I make a couple of trips to the blockade on the weekend, though I don't exactly spend all my spare time making small talk with Matt and Granny. To be honest, I'm still quite angry with both of them.

At home, it's really weird, ominously quiet. Whenever we sit down to eat, the ghosts of Matt and Granny seem to be sitting with us. I wonder if there is such a thing as a living ghost, if parts of Matt and Granny want to be at home with us, sipping turkey rice soup while it's still piping hot.

On Wednesday after school, when Dad and I are out at the camp dropping off a giant tarp—the original tarp isn't big enough to cover the swelling ranks of protesters—I see Karin. I duck down in the truck cab, but it's too late. She has already spotted me.

Not only does she come over to the truck, she does it with her camera turned on and pointed right at me. "Tell me what you are doing here," she shouts through the closed window.

"Delivering food," I yell back.

I stare at the dashboard and hope she will vaporize. Of course, she doesn't. She rolls her hand around in the air, gesturing for me to open the window.

I stare harder at the dashboard and she raps on the glass. I still ignore her but she's persistent. She doesn't ask a third time and I nearly fall right out onto the gravel when she yanks the door open.

"What are you doing?"

"Trying to interview you. You aren't very cooperative."

"No comment."

"Very funny."

"I'm not trying to be funny."

"How do you feel about the police presence?"

"What kind of question is that?"

"Are you concerned that your relatives might be arrested?"

I figure I'd better answer, or I'm going to seem like a real idiot. "Of course I am. Wouldn't you be?" The camera's red light is on—she's recording everything I say and do. Who knows where she's going to show the stupid film? "Don't you have to ask permission before you film someone?"

Karin holds the camera to the side but keeps filming. "You're out in public. What you do here is in a public place—I can film you."

"I'm in a private vehicle."

"On a public road. Police photograph bad drivers and

their licence plates all the time."

I'd rather eat a whole can of olives, which I despise, than let know-it-all Karin have the last word.

"Are you going to put this conversation in the movie? To show how you harass innocent citizens?"

Karin jerks the camera down. "Fine. If that's how you feel. But like it or not, the film would be better with you in it."

It must kill her to say that. I'm sure she likes me about as much as I like olives.

"Let me know if you change your mind." Karin turns away and lifts the camera. She aims it at the circle of women gathered around the steel fire barrel.

Someone yells, but nothing exciting happens. It's just one protester yelling at another protester to find out whether or not she wants honey in her ginseng tea.

The truck's door is still open and as I watch Karin moving toward the fire, I reach for the handle to pull it shut. But some part of my brain intervenes. I don't want to sit in the stupid truck alone waiting for something to happen or Dad to drive me home.

I grab my notebook and pen and hop out. It takes only a moment to sum up the options for direction of travel:

a. *Toward the steel burning barrel. Not an option. Old ladies and Karin.*
b. *Down the road. Not an option. Police cars and angry loggers.*
c. *Up the road. Not an option. Steep hill.*

Which leaves a path just ahead of the truck on the opposite side of the road from the camp. The trail leads slightly downhill (good!) and away from all the crazy people (even better!) and disappears into heavy brush under the trees (perfect—I won't have to go far before I'm out of sight).

19

The essence of drama is that man cannot walk away from the consequences of his own deeds. –Harold Hayes

When we lived in Ontario we spent our summers at my grandparents' farm. Most of the land was cleared, planted in corn or hay or used for grazing a small herd of dairy cows.

There was one part of the land that had never been farmed. It was a gully that ran along the south side of the property. This was the only place where anything like a forest grew. Huge old maples, some willows along the bottom near the creek, some tall, stick-thin alders. That part of the farm was where Matt and I built a treehouse, played cowboys and wild horse roundup, and made stick boats to float down the stream.

When we first moved to Tarragon Island, I didn't like the forests here. The Ontario gully was bright and sunny and there was plenty of space between the trees. Here, the forests are dark. The trees are huge and close together. They rise up and up and up and in places their branches make a canopy so thick you can barely see the sky. The first time I went for a walk it was creepy, the kind of strange world you'd expect to find in a horror movie. I imagined werewolves or sasquatches or bears or at least evil spirits would feel perfectly at home among the moss-wrapped trees with trunks so huge a dozen or more people could join hands in a circle around them.

But then I got to know the island trees a little better. Our own stand of cedars at home is a perfect place to hide from irritating younger brothers or parents who have a knack for finding odd jobs to keep a person busy on a lazy summer afternoon.

So I'm not afraid of the forest any more and today, just like at home, the trees are a welcome retreat from people I don't want to deal with. As I wind my way along the path, the noises of the camp fade. At first, I'm watchful, wary, keep glancing behind me to see if anyone has followed me. I trot down a small hill and around another bend, and then the quiet is complete.

I slow down, moving easily through the tall trees draped in old man's beard, the strange, pale green lichen that hangs from branches like a wild imitation of Christmas garlands. A path like this is addictive, enticing. One more bend and another few trees and then another curve and then the sound backdrop changes. If I stand still and hold my breath I can hear a hiss or whisper, like a long sigh, and a few more steps confirm that somewhere ahead is running water.

As I get closer, the water sounds become more distinct and I can tease out burbles, trickles, and swooshes. I scramble up over a small rise and there it is, a shallow stream split into half a dozen rivulets that skip and dance right over the path. Scattered rocks and boulders, some larger than I am, interrupt the water's flow and create pools, eddies, and gurgling swirls. It smells sweeter, somehow, right here beside the water, and I stop, close my eyes, and draw in a deep breath. It feels so good to be away from the noise of the camp, the smells of smoke and roasting veggie dogs.

"Don't be startled."

My notebook flies out of my hand and my pen rolls into the stream as I leap straight into the air and spin around to face the voice.

"I'm so sorry, dear. I didn't mean to scare you." The old woman sits on a wooden bench facing the stream before she adds, "You're one of them from the road, are you?"

"No. Not really. My grandmother—"

She raises her hand and silences me, then gestures across the stream. I turn away from her and it takes a minute to see what she's pointing at. Something moves and then I spot it—a squirrel scampering along a branch leaps into a neighbouring tree and disappears around behind the trunk.

"I'm glad they're here," she says, and it takes me a moment to realize she's talking about protesters and not squirrels. "Though it will be better when they go away."

Turning back to face her I realize my initial assumption that she is one of the Ladies of the Forest could not have been right. She wears a dirty cotton head scarf and a torn red-and-black-checked man's lumberjack shirt over a knitted sweater. A ratty skirt over some kind of leggings is covered by an apron with large pockets. The pockets bulge, though I can't see what's inside. Judging by the wrinkles creasing her brown skin she must be a hundred years old. She makes Granny look like a spring chicken.

"So you're not a protester?"

She doesn't answer right away. "I was born here."

"Really?"

"Hmm." Her eyes fill with tears and she reaches into an apron pocket for a rumpled handkerchief she uses to dab at her eyes. I turn away and search for my pen in the stream and then pick up my notebook. I move slowly, deliberately, giving the old woman plenty of time to recover. When I finally turn back to her, the bench is empty.

"Over here," she says. "Would you like to see where I was born?"

It isn't so much a question as a command. She is already moving away from me through the trees, silent, like a ghost. I have no choice. I follow.

We wind along, roughly parallel to the stream, and after ten minutes or so, emerge onto the logging road at a point I assume to be well past the camp. There's no sign of any protesters. I can't even hear the drums.

A short way along and on the other side of the road the old woman picks up the trail again. All this time, she says nothing. The trail begins to climb and soon we are moving through a different kind of forest. There are no giant cedars here. All the trees are the same—tall and straight but at the same time scraggly looking compared to the forest we left on the other side of the road.

The old woman moves on, steady and sure, sometimes moving around fallen trees, sometimes stepping over them. There isn't really a trail any more but the woman seems to know exactly where she is going. I glance behind me but the trees have closed in. There is no sign of the road. No landmarks. For better or worse I am really stuck with the old woman now.

The next fifteen minutes are agony, not because the trek is hard; it isn't. My guide is easy enough to keep up with. But I'm beginning to worry that Dad will notice I'm missing. It's hard to know exactly how long I've been gone. How will I explain that I've been abducted by an ancient woman who did nothing more than ask a question and start walking? Why had I followed? Not to be rude? Out of morbid curiosity? Boredom? All of the above?

It's brighter ahead and when we step beyond the edge of the forest it's as if someone has punched me hard in the gut.

And lo, the valley of death lay spread before me.

The devastation is total. Blackened stumps and charred earth stretch away through a shallow valley and creep partway up the slopes of the surrounding hills. Nothing moves across this wasteland and nothing could compel me to take even one step into it.

"Was it a forest fire?"

"Forest fire? No." The old woman shakes her head slowly from side to side. "This is what they do after they clear-cut a forest. They burn anything they can't sell. They say it enriches the soil." She lets out a short laugh and shakes her head again. "Enriches the soil, my ass."

Looking at the moonscape before us I can't imagine anything will ever grow there again.

"I was born in a cabin in this forest." Her gaze is fixed on a point somewhere out there in the middle of the clear-cut.

"This is your land?"

"All of this was once our land," she says quietly. "Nobody ever paid my grandfather for it. They ignored the cabin for some years but one day my father had to buy a piece on the other side of the road, down by the stream where I first saw you. My father wanted to buy this land, his own land, back from the government. But he couldn't afford it all, even if they would have sold it to him."

She turns and retraces her steps without saying another word.

We cross the road, with me following a few steps behind as if we're still on a narrow path. Before I know it, we are back at the bench by the stream.

"Homework?" she asks, pulling a cigarette from a pocket in her plaid shirt. She waves her other hand at my notebook.

"No, not really. Kind of."

She lights up, takes a deep drag, and then turns and walks away, leaving me standing there as if she's lost interest in making conversation.

When she disappears along the edge of the stream I turn and sprint back up the trail to the camp. It takes longer than I remember and more of the trail is uphill than I would have guessed, so I'm sweaty, flushed, and out of breath when I trot into the food tent and ask for Dad.

"I think he's still visiting with your grandmother," Mrs. Lalli says. "Check over by her tent."

"Dad!"

"Heather! There you are. Ready to go?"

"No."

Granny, Matt, and Dad stare at me as if something bizarre is growing out of my ear.

"Have you seen Karin?"

"The nice girl with the camera?" Granny asks, and I can barely bother to feel prickly at her suggestion that Karin is "nice."

"Yeah. Her."

"Maybe where they're singing? Just down the road."

"Thanks."

And before I've even properly caught my breath I sprint off to find her. Her movie will not be complete without footage of the clear-cut and the old woman who used to live there.

20

True ease in writing comes from art, not chance,
As those move easiest who have learn'd to dance.
'Tis not enough no harshness gives offence,–
The sound must seem an echo to the sense.

– Alexander Pope

The next day I spend quite a lot of time working on another article for the paper, not even trying to be balanced and impartial. How can I be when I'm living inside the story? Most of my lunch hour is spent in the library, doing research on the computer.

What I really want to do is understand, really understand, why the protesters are doing what they are doing and why the forestry companies keep clear-cutting when everyone seems to agree that clear-cutting is pretty unhealthy. But I keep getting bogged down with questions I can't find answers to by myself.

Which is why, after school, I ask Dad if I can come along when he takes the big water containers to the Tarragon Woods.

"Are you saying that you are voluntarily going to speak

with your grandmother?"

"As a matter of fact, yes. And probably some of the other women, too."

The drive goes quickly. Dad hums along with the radio and I count telephone poles.

At least, it goes quickly until we come up the hill after the creek and run straight into a roadblock. No protesters, just two police cars, one pointing in each direction, lights twirling.

"Oh, no," Dad says. "This doesn't look good." He pulls over to the side of the road when an officer waves a glowing orange stick at him.

"Good afternoon, sir. Can I ask where you might be going?"

"To the protest camp up the road. Is that okay?"

A second police officer walks around to the back of the truck and reads the licence plate number into a hand-held radio.

"What would your purpose be in going to the camp?"

"To visit my mother-in-law."

"Are you intending to join the protest?"

"You know, I think this is a public road, right?"

I feel sweat prickling under my sweater. What is he doing? It's not a good idea to argue with the police.

"We have a situation up ahead, sir."

"What kind of a situation? Peaceful citizens involved in a peaceful protest is no reason—"

"Dad." I tug on his sleeve and he shrugs his arm away from me.

"Sir. If you insist on going any farther, I'm going to have to ask you to leave your vehicle—"

She doesn't finish whatever she was going to say because right then her radio crackles and she and the second officer turn together and stride away from us toward the barricade erected across the road.

"What the—"

"Dad—just wait to see what they say."

Dad hunches forward over the wheel and for one scary moment I have this dreadful feeling that he's going to hit the gas and drive forward at top speed. Just like in the movies the police officers will scatter out of the way, the orange cones and the barricades will smash, and then gunshots will blow out our back windshield as we careen around the corner, rebels to the end.

Dad takes a deep breath, leans back, and shifts the truck out of drive. He turns up the country music station and hums along with a song about a rodeo clown who has lost the will to live.

We watch as the police officers talk into their radios, listen, and nod. Occasionally one of them glances at us, but mostly they seem intent on giving or receiving instructions of some sort.

"Maybe we could come back later?" I say.

"I don't think they can stop us from going to visit the camp."

I'm certainly not going to point out that we have already been stopped. Who knows how long it will be before they open the road again.

"Don't you think it sounded like maybe we could walk

up there? We could come back for the water later."

Dad cranes his neck around to see behind us. "This is a terrible place for a roadblock. It's hardly wide enough for two vehicles to pass, never mind for someone to park. Maybe if we back down the road a bit . . ."

I don't think Dad would appreciate it if I pointed out that a narrow spot in the road is the perfect place for a roadblock, so I keep my mouth shut and my eyes on the police.

He is just about to put the truck in reverse when one of the officers comes trotting toward us. "Dad! Wait a minute."

The officer gestures to the narrow dirt strip beside the gravel that serves as the shoulder of the road. The second officer hauls away the barrier.

"Is the road open?" I ask, but the first officer is pointing at the side of the road. It's perfectly clear that she wants us to pull over. Up close, I can see just how big her gun is. Dad must notice, too, because he meekly drives to the side of the road.

We have hardly moved out of the way when a school bus rumbles around the corner from the direction of the camp followed by dozens of protesters who are yelling and screaming and bashing at the sides of the bus with placards. Several spots on the front and sides bear black-and-white signs saying POLICE.

As the procession of bus, motorcycle escorts, and furious protesters rumbles past, I notice something else. At each window a face peers out and palms press flat against the glass, handcuff chains swinging beneath them. One young woman with a scarf over her head is crying and looks like a refugee. Most of the passengers are women and many of the woman are older. But in a seat toward the back I see a familiar face that makes my stomach turn.

"Matt!" I scream. "Mattie!!" Dad isn't quick enough to stop me from jumping out of the truck and sprinting along after the bus. I run down the road, my arms pumping, my feet pounding into the gravel, screaming at the retreating bus. Soon, only a couple of young men are still running with me. After the bus winds its way around one more turn it disappears and, defeated, we have to stop. Gasping for air, I turn and head back up the hill. I don't have to go far before our truck appears and Dad slows down long enough for me to scramble up into the cab.

"Unbelievable," he says. "This is Canada, for God's sake. We don't throw children in jail!" Then he hits the gas, spinning the tires so fast that gravel spits out in all directions.

21

From the sublime to the ridiculous is but a step.

— Napoleon Bonaparte

The Tarragon Island police station is a boring-looking concrete and brick box just outside Rosehip, but as we pull into the parking lot, my palms start to sweat. "Maybe we shouldn't go in," I say.

"What are you talking about? They have Mattie in there!"

"Could we get arrested?"

"Why would they arrest us? We haven't done anything wrong."

"What about Matt? He's ten years old. What could he possibly have done wrong?"

"Maybe he did something foolish—like threw a rock or a bottle at the police."

The way Dad says it, I know he doesn't believe for a minute that our Matt would do anything like that. Dad shakes his head and yanks the key out of the ignition.

"I cannot believe we are having this conversation. We don't live in a war zone. This is not the Middle East."

Bewildered. Furious. Helpless. That's how Dad sounds and it makes me shiver, as though someone has just walked over my grave.

We run into the building and up to the reception desk.

"Hi, my name is Ben Blake. I think you have my son here?"

"Are you talking about one of the protesters? They're still on the bus out in the loading bay. It will take a while to process everyone."

"Look, there must be some mistake. Matt is only ten. He was with his grandmother. Can I see him?"

"Sir, I'm afraid we have to do the paperwork for each person we bring in. I'm sure your son is fine."

"You don't even know if my son is on that bus, do you?"

The receptionist looks at Dad over her half-glasses. "Sir, I understand you are concerned—"

"Concerned!" Dad's fist bangs on the counter. "Let me see my boy!"

The woman regards Dad, taking in his bulging eyes, the vein throbbing at his temple. "Social Services has been called."

"Social Services?" Dad sputters as the woman raises her hand.

"Standard procedure when young children are in trouble with the law."

Dad draws in a sharp breath and I reach out to touch his arm.

"Dad," I whisper. Nothing he could say at this point

would be helpful.

Thankfully, the phone rings and the woman puts up a finger before Dad can speak. "Yes, sir—I'll put you through." She presses another button and then raises an eyebrow at Dad.

I can tell by the way he is pinching the bottom of his coat zipper between his thumb and forefinger that he is getting really mad, so I'm pretty impressed when he calmly asks, "Would you mind checking to see if Matthew Blake is on that bus? My daughter thought she saw him, but she only had a glimpse, and—"

"Just a moment," she says as she gets up and disappears through a door beyond her desk. The door clicks shut behind her and we can barely make out her voice talking to someone. She returns a minute later and gives Dad a curt nod.

"They have him. As I said, he'll be taken in to see a social worker."

"Social worker? Can I see him? How long will that take?"

"Well, the social worker normally comes to the island only on Mondays and Wednesdays."

"But it's Thursday! You can't keep him here all weekend!"

"Sir, please. Under the circumstances, we've put in an emergency request. The social worker has already been contacted and will be on the next ferry from Victoria. You'll be able to see Matthew after he has had a chance to be counselled."

"Counselled! He doesn't need to be counselled. What's

wrong with you people? I'm calling a lawyer! Don't you dare touch him until—"

The door at the back swings open and the woman police officer from the roadblock comes through, pushing a strand of stray hair back out of her eyes.

"Is it true you are keeping children locked up in here?" Dad demands to know.

"I know this is difficult," she says in a kindly voice. "What is your name?"

"Ben. Ben Blake. Matt is my son." Dad's voice quavers and I look up to see if he's crying.

"Mr. Blake, your son refused to leave the road and we had no choice but to move him. But he wasn't arrested."

All the blood drains from Dad's face. "What? Then why—"

"There were several children taken into temporary custody. I can release him into your care if you have some photo identification."

"That's it? What about—" Dad looks at the receptionist and then turns back to the police officer. "Yes. Yes, I have identification."

"If you give your information to Allison and then have a seat, I'll be right back."

"Right back" turns out to be an endless half-hour during which Dad looks at his watch thirty-seven times. I know because I count each quick twist of his wrist.

Finally, the door behind the reception desk swings open and the police officer appears with Matt. Matt's wearing a huge brown and yellow sweater at least three sizes too big for him. His cheeks are streaky and he's filthy. He doesn't run over to Dad and leap into his arms the way I think I would. He walks slowly with a stiff deliberation as if to say that he will not be bothered by everything he's been through.

Matt maintains his composure through a long hug from Dad, a punch in the shoulder from me, and all the way across the parking lot. But when he is in the back seat, his hands are shaking so badly he can't get his seat belt done up. I lean over to help and that's when a single tear escapes and trickles down his cheek.

"Wow, Matt," I say. "I never thought you'd turn out to be, like, a gangster." The smallest hint of a smile lifts the corner of his mouth and then he turns his head to the window and stares outside. He doesn't say a word all the way home. Neither does Dad. I study my hands, wishing I could think of a great joke, or something profound.

We are halfway home when I realize that Dad never even checked to see if Granny was on that bus. I almost ask Matt, but his forehead is glued to the window and I'm a little worried that the question might make him have some sort of traumatic breakdown.

As it turns out, I don't have to wait long to find out about Granny. Mom is waiting for us at home, ready with a big hug and a cup of hot chocolate for Matt and a grim message for all of us. Granny was arrested. This time they aren't planning to let her out so easily.

"What do you mean, they won't let her out this time? They can't keep her locked up forever," Dad says.

"No—not forever. But she has refused to sign some form promising to stay away from the logging road. So, they are threatening to charge her with contempt of court as well as public mischief."

"What does all that mean?" I ask.

Mom and Dad exchange worried glances. "I don't understand all the legal ins and outs," Mom says, "but the contempt of court thing sounds pretty serious, if she's found guilty. We'll know more tomorrow. A lawyer is coming over from Victoria to represent several protesters who have refused to cooperate."

"Wow. I can't believe this is happening."

"Neither can I, Heather. Neither can I."

22

Your manuscript is both good and original, but the part that is good is not original, and the part that is original is not good. – Samuel Johnson

I don't really want to go to the writing group the following Thursday, but in the same way that the rest of the week unfolds even though I don't want any part of it, I find myself walking in the door in time for the meeting.

Willow and Wynd arrive, and Karin is so excited about getting her videotape into the machine she doesn't even wait until they're settled into their seats. "Can I go first?"

Eric glances around and since nobody else seems to want to go first, he nods. "Sure, I guess so."

"Heather, I didn't get a chance to edit the clear-cut footage. But thanks, I got some really good stuff." She flashes me a quick, warm smile and presses the *play* button.

This time the film is exciting right from the very first frame. I don't even know if that's the right terminology. I don't think digital video cameras, or whatever they're called, shoot in frames, but that's how Karin puts it.

"Pay attention to the opening scene!"

I have to hand it to her, it is good. Captivating. There is footage of an old woman who is shaking her fist in front of the grille of a massive logging truck. The driver of the truck leans out the open window and screams obscenities at her. She screams right back, but she's not swearing. She's shouting sayings like "Save our trees!" and "It's all about the money!" Several other women run up behind her, gather around, take her arms in theirs, and pull her away.

Then we see the revolving red and blue lights on top of a police car. An officer gets out of the car with one hand on the butt of his pistol. The woman who had been in front of the truck breaks free from the others, who are trying to keep her away from the driver. She dodges past her friends and rips open the door of the truck.

"Don't be a coward! Be a man! Come out here and discuss this with us."

"What's there to discuss?" he yells back at her, waving his fist. "You aren't here to discuss anything. You crazy ladies are just here to ruin my business!" The man is bright red in the face and he's leaning out of the truck. "I have kids to feed, you self-centred idiot! Don't you understand that?"

"Of course, I understand that. I have children, too. That's why I'm here, I have grandchildren and one great-granddaughter. But if we destroy our environment, what will be left for future generations?"

"I'm not destroying the environment! Trees grow

back—look at all those trees back down the road a way. That forest was cut only a hundred years ago."

"Exactly! Do you see any great old cedars here? Of course not. Those ancient beauties are long gone. Nobody here will ever see them again."

The scene suddenly cuts off. We all lean forward toward the TV, anxious to know what happens next. My heart thuds and I have to move my tongue around to generate some saliva. It must have been terrifying to watch the confrontation. It's bad enough seeing it on tape.

"So did the truck, like, drive over the old lady?"

Karin doesn't answer so Wynd keeps going. "Is that why you stopped filming?"

"I would have kept filming for sure if someone got run over," Willow adds.

Karin pushes buttons to rewind and eject the videotape. "Nobody got run over."

"That's why the police are there," Gillian says. "To keep everybody safe."

"Yeah, right," I say.

"That's what the police do," Gillian insists.

"Keep everybody safe?" I say, my heart leaping away. "From a bunch of wild grandmothers and little kids? Give me a break. The police are there to arrest the protesters."

"Heather's right," Karin says. "What rock have you been hiding under all week, Gillian? It's true that the police asked the trucker to back off. And they also made sure the women got out of the way so they didn't get run over. But the same police officers put handcuffs on

Heather's grandmother and lifted her into a police car when she wouldn't walk."

"I don't mean to be rude," Gillian says, obviously uncomfortable but determined to make her point. "But your grandmother did something illegal."

Much as I like Gillian, I lose it. "Excuse me? The last time that I checked, Canada was a democracy. I do believe that a democracy allows its citizens the right to protest in a peaceful manner."

Eric nods but he also raises an eyebrow in my direction.

"Please forgive me if there's another Heather Blake on this island who writes articles for the newspaper," Gillian says, her bottom lip quivering. "Aren't you the one who said the Ladies of the Forest had no right to stop other people from going to work?"

I could throw something at her. A poisoned dart. Or maybe a hammer. Just wait until she reads the next article, the one due out in next week's paper. "For personal reasons maybe I don't like what my grandmother is doing. But throwing her in jail like someone who committed a murder or drove a car after a dozen beers or beat up their kids or whatever isn't right. Besides, she's an old lady!"

"So being old makes it okay to break the law?"

I know Gillian has a point, but I'm so mad I yell, "What do you know about the law, anyway?! You just write stupid stories about talking animals!"

Which is when a single tear trickles down Gillian's cheek.

The complete and utter silence in the room feels like someone poured a million litres of water over all of us. Nobody seems to know where to look. In desperation, we all turn to Eric.

He throws his hands up as if he's protecting his face from an attack. "What did I do?" There's something so funny about the way he flings himself backwards that Karin bursts out laughing.

"Oh, my God—is your group always this exciting?" Karin asks.

"Gillian, I'm sorry. I like your stories. I shouldn't have said that."

"Yeah, not exactly constructive criticism, Blake." For some dumb reason, when Eric says this it strikes us as terribly funny and the next thing I know we are all falling over laughing.

"And did you see Custer?" Eric giggles.

"Yes!" Willow squeals. "You looked hilarious! Like someone watching a crazy Ping-Pong game!"

Dutifully, Custer raises his eyebrows and sends his eyes bouncing back and forth, back and forth. This causes such a reaction he makes his two forefingers bop up and down and back and forth as if they are dancing or playing some crazy game.

"Stop!" I wheeze, wiping tears from my cheeks. "I can't breathe!"

The others are just as badly off and by the time we compose ourselves our earlier harsh words have receded.

"I'm sorry," I say again, and Gillian gives a small nod in acknowledgement.

"We should get back to work here," Eric says. Then he looks at me and asks, "You didn't write anything about . . . about, you know . . ."

"Protesters? Loggers? What, are you crazy?" They can read what I have to say about the war in the woods along with everyone else on the island when the paper comes out.

"That's a relief," says Karin with a giggle, and strangely enough, even though I feel as though I should still be angry, I laugh too. Then I pull out my notebook and read a character sketch about a carpenter who includes a hidden compartment or secret space or passage in every house he builds.

23

Writing is a lot easier if you have something to say.

— Sholem Asch

"Good morning, Heather."

Being greeted by a tight-lipped principal as I reach to push open the front door at school is not a good omen.

"Let's go into my office, shall we?"

Shall we? Something about the way Mrs. Gurney hurries me into her office sets my heart racing. What now?

"Wait here. We have another situation with your locker."

I sink into the chair opposite Mrs. Gurney's desk. Great. The door closes behind her and I'm left alone in the principal's private domain. Mrs. Gurney's desk is spotless, nearly empty except for a phone, a box of tissues, a toffee tin full of pens and pencils, and my article in today's paper.

It's silly to feel guilty for turning it around so I can read it, but I keep glancing up at the door as I skim the familiar words, almost as jumpy as if I'm looking at Mrs. Gurney's private diary.

Police State Victimizes Children and Grandmothers

By Heather Blake

In a world where criminals are released from jail after making secret deals or get off with a slap on the wrist, how is it fair that innocent citizens who are exercising the right to peaceful protest get thrown into jail?

In this country, even children aren't safe from our overenthusiastic police. Did you know that last week twenty-two people were arrested on Lower Tarragon Road? These so-called criminals included two teenagers and two children, one as young as ten years old. What did this little boy do to deserve a terrifying trip to our local jail? He stood on a road with his arms crossed and sang. When police asked him to move, he and the others sat down. When they tried to make him stand up, he went all floppy. Now I know from experience how annoying it is when my little brother goes all floppy and uncooperative, but is that any reason to arrest him?

Yes, that is exactly what happened last week. While he was on the bus, a police officer brought in from Victoria told the teenagers that they might be taken away from their parents, that their parents could be charged with neglect under the law. Can you imagine how overhearing that conversation made the boy feel?

Our teachers are always telling us to get involved with the political process, to learn about issues that affect us, and then to take responsibility for our future. But what happens when a young boy actually tries to do that by learning about the forest and logging methods and then standing up for what he believes in? It doesn't matter whether or not you agree with what the protesters are saying, no child should have to experience the trauma this young boy did. The logging companies are wrong to attack the protesters like this; they are nothing more than impatient, unthinking brutes. I know that one driver threatened an old lady with his truck. How is that a fair fight? Why are these trees the only ones they can cut down? Why don't they go somewhere else and chop somebody else's trees down?

I am embarrassed to be a citizen of an island where these things can happen.

I hope someone takes a copy to Granny in jail. It might cheer her up. Because she still won't sign the paper promising to stay away from the loggers, she's been locked up in jail ever since her latest arrest. Nearly two weeks without decent coffee: she's not a happy jailbird. The cell here on the island really isn't designed for long-term visitors, so today they're moving her to another jail over in Victoria where she will have to wait for some hearing with a judge who will decide what to do with her. Maybe the coffee will be better in the big city.

Finally, Mrs. Gurney comes back and lowers herself into her leather swivel chair.

"Oh, Heather—I thought things had settled down after your other article."

What am I supposed to say to that? The cap kids had been ignoring me, that much is true. But some of the kids from greeny families have been disturbingly rude.

And someone in my family always seems to hate what I have to say.

"Do you think this was wise?" Mrs. Gurney touches the edge of the paper and pushes it toward me. She says it like I'm trying to make trouble. "Heather?"

I don't want to say anything. I've said enough in my articles.

"Heather." She talks more slowly now, carefully folding her lips around each word. "Do you think this was wise?" She leans forward, challenging me, wanting me to say, *No. It was stupid. Dumb, dumb Heather—what was she thinking?*

The words that shoot back at her surprise us both. "My brother was hauled off to jail like a lowly criminal. Do you think that was wise?"

Mrs. Gurney draws her hand back and drums her fingers on the edge of her desk before she speaks again. "Heather, I know you must be very upset about what happened. But calling the loggers—where is that bit—oh, here, *impatient, unthinking brutes.* I can't protect you here at school. I had two messages on my phone this morning when I came in."

I wonder if they are like the calls we've had at the house from heavy breathers who say things like "Keep your nose out of our business. We have chainsaws," and then hang up. They call from pay phones or cellphones with the numbers blocked so there's no way to trace them through the call display.

"And your locker . . ."

She doesn't elaborate and I don't press her for details.

I don't want to know what they've done to my locker this time.

"I'm sorry."

"It's not me you need to apologize to. A lot of people here are upset about what happened at the blockade. But the law is the law and all of the protesters understood that they might be arrested if they continued to block the road. And your parents should never have—"

The phone rings and she snatches up the receiver. "Mrs. Gurney speaking. Yes—yes, I'm aware of that. Thank you. Let her know I'll call her back shortly."

She drops the receiver back into the cradle and leans toward me, her elbows on the desk, her fingers interlaced. "What are we going to do?"

What I want to do is go to sleep for a very long time, long enough that everyone will just forget about my articles, the trees, my grandmother. "Can't I just go to class?"

"I think we need to give people some time to cool off. I need to contact some parents, have a word with a few students. And maybe this isn't the best place for you to be while all that is happening. The police will be here soon to investigate. We can't ignore this."

"The police?" I don't know what to think about the police any more. Whose side will they be on? Will they blame me for aggravating people? "But I didn't do it on purpose to make people mad."

She nods. "I know. Sorry, that's not what I meant. The police are coming to investigate the threats, the phone calls. You aren't in trouble."

If I'm not in trouble, then why am I about to burst into tears? Why does it sound as though the principal is sending me home?

"Am I, like, suspended?" I can hardly get the word out.

"Oh, Heather—I am so sorry you're all caught up in this mess. No, you are not suspended. And I can't forbid you from coming to school. But I would recommend that you stay home for a few days. I'll escort you to your locker if you need any books and of course I'll let your teachers know. You may use my phone to call home and have someone come to pick you up. Will that be a problem?"

I shake my head and then shake it again when she asks if I need to go to my locker. I have enough to get by with at home and in my backpack.

"I'll give you some privacy to make your call."

Mrs. Gurney waits with me outside the front of the school until Dad arrives in the truck. I jump in as he gets out to have a few words with Mrs. Gurney. Inside the truck I close my eyes and pretend I am somewhere very far away.

Writer Girl swoops low over the dust of the red planet, searching for the nest of abaloids she spotted on her last reconnaissance flight. Her jet pack sputters and she curses. "What? No fuel?? What a place to perish . . ."

"Well, I never thought one of my children would be arrested and the other kicked out of school all in the same month."

It's a dumb joke, but I manage a weak smile.

"What a mess," he adds. "What a damned mess."

He doesn't say much else on the way home, and I'm just as happy that I don't have to make idle conversation. In my mind I zip back to the mysterious red planet and fantasize about the various ways that Writer Girl is going to get herself out of her dire predicament.

"So what was it like in the slammer?" Uma presses.

"Leave him alone. Maybe he doesn't want to talk about it."

"I think he can talk for himself. He's been in jail. That makes anybody tough."

"What do you know? Have you ever been in jail?"

"I'm not talking to you."

Alyssum sits beside Matt. "It's okay. You don't have to talk about it."

"I wasn't really in jail," he says. "Not really. The kids were only in the jail cell for a little while. It was pretty crowded."

"What happens if you have to pee? Do you have to press a buzzer or something until they let you out?"

"There's a toilet right in the cell. It's more like a big room. It has a solid door. No bars."

"What if one person hogs the bathroom and won't come out?"

"There are no walls around the toilet."

"What?!" Alyssum and Uma pull faces at each other.

"Ewww . . . I could never go in front of other people.

Is there a curtain or anything?"

Matt is warming up to this appreciative audience. "Curtain? No. Just this metal toilet—"

"Metal?" Alyssum squeaks. "Chilly!"

"Yeah, especially since there's no toilet seat."

"What!? How do you, you know, do number two?"

"Squat, I guess. I told you I wasn't in there long enough to find out."

"But what about all those other people? How many were in there? How big is the cell? Are there bunk beds? Where do people sleep?"

"Most of the protesters didn't stay for long. Only those who refused to sign the forms had to stay overnight and then the really serious offenders—"

"Like your grandmother?" Uma interrupts, obviously relishing every last gory detail of my criminal family's capture and incarceration.

"Yes, like Granny. The people who had been previously arrested had to go to Victoria. Granny moved today. I think there is another lady, too—another Lady of the Forest. They have to wait for a hearing in court."

Uma shakes her head. "This is so amazing. This is just like the story of Gandhi. He stuck with his cause, stood up for what he believed in, no matter what the consequences."

"It's not like that at all," I say.

"Sure it is. I bet if enough people get arrested they will have to stop cutting down the trees. I think Matt is a hero." Uma smiles sweetly at Matt, and Alyssum actually rubs his back. He doesn't even squirm out of the way. It's really quite revolting.

"Can we please get on with our meeting?" I say. "I don't have all night."

"It's not like you have to get up and go to school," Matt points out.

"I have homework anyway. And besides, tomorrow night is the writing group and I'm working on some stuff that I want to read."

"More po-ee-tree?"

"Oh, be quiet. I don't write much poetry these days."

"Can't handle the rejection letters?"

Hero or not, I land on top of Matt and give him a good poke in the ribs. He lets out a squeal and the four of us find ourselves in a spontaneous tickle knot where everyone is tickling everyone until nobody can breathe.

When we've recovered we set to work designing reading project posters to put up in schools and down at the bandshell in the park. There's a round bulletin board under a cedar-shake roof where everyone posts notices about everything imaginable. Somebody always knows somebody who saw a notice for the perfect breeding ram or used computer desk or pile of scrap lumber. The feed store on Green Valley Road has a good notice board and so does the grocery store. Soon we have a list of twenty places on the island that need posters and a list just as long of people we have to phone or visit.

Considering the level of enthusiasm in the room, the others don't give me too much trouble about the fact I haven't yet submitted the reading story to the paper. I add it to my mental list of things I have to get written and inwardly groan. What must it be like to be a full-time professional writer? Way more stressful than I ever would have imagined! Now I understand why Eugene Ionesco said, "A writer never has a vacation. For a writer, life consists of either writing or thinking about writing." I wonder what this Ionesco guy wrote. That's the problem with the quotes I find—most of the time I don't have a clue who these people are. Not that it matters—he's right. Being a writer, or even thinking about being a writer, is a full-time job.

24

My most important piece of advice to all you would-be writers: when you write, try to leave out all the parts readers skip. – Elmore Leonard

"Who wants to go first?"

Gillian pulls out a thick sheaf of papers and starts riffling the pages, searching for something. "I'll go."

Good. Gillian's cute talking-animal stories are usually pretty entertaining. But this week, there are no animals anywhere in what Gillian has brought. Instead, she reads a copy of a letter she has sent to the editor at the paper, and listening to her read it aloud is about as pleasant as being in the shower when someone flushes the toilet downstairs.

"Dear Editor,

I am writing in response to recent articles published in your newspaper about the Ladies of the Forest and the arrests of the protesters in the Tarragon Woods. I don't think it's right that you print articles like the one by Heather Blake because this is not good reporting. Even though you put the article on the opinion page, some people might think that this writer actually knows what she's talking about. She does not.

The only people who are breaking the law are the protesters. No logger has hurt a protester and it isn't against the law to get mad at someone who is stopping you from going to work. To keep bringing up the ages of some of the people who are going to jail is irrelevant and just makes people mad and they forget what the real problem is: people are defying the law and refusing to cooperate with police.

While I agree that ten years old is a bit young to be arrested for something like this (because I don't think ten-year-olds are old enough to understand what they are doing—the boy mentioned in the article must have been under the influence of an adult), somebody should be responsible for this boy's actions since it's clear he isn't responsible for himself. Where are his parents? My parents would never let me put myself in danger like this. I think his parents are the ones who should be arrested. I do feel sorry for what this boy had to go through, but I feel even more sorry that he lives in a family that doesn't even care enough about him to keep him safe.

I hope you print this letter. Yours sincerely, Gillian Wong."

Never once during the whole letter does Gillian look up. When she finishes, she slides the letter back into the folder and stares down at the toes of her red slippers. Our usually rambunctious group is deathly silent. Only Eric risks a quick glance in my direction. Everyone else is suddenly interested in the spiral wires binding their notebooks, the clicking mechanism of their pens, the ceiling. We sit there for a really long time, and with every second that passes it seems more impossible for anyone to say anything.

I want to cheer when Karin gets up with a videotape in her hand and heads for the television set. The strangest feeling of gratitude comes over me: it's a good thing that Karin is out there pointing her camera in everyone's face, recording what's *really* going on. I almost wish I'd had more to say to her out there on the logging road.

Everyone follows Karin's every movement as she puts in the tape, as if her actions are the most fascinating and entertaining thing we have ever seen.

Still without saying a word, she returns to her place on the couch and we stare, transfixed, at the images on the screen, as though we are watching a hideous car crash or a skydiver leaping from an airplane with a faulty parachute.

Matt's face fills the screen. He's wearing a knitted blue toque pulled way down over his ears. He looks grubby, like someone who has been camping, but happy at the same time. His cheeks are flushed red and his eyes twinkle as he sings, "Our roots dig down, down, down into our Mother Earth."

The camera pulls back and we see that Matt is surrounded by other people, mostly women, who are all singing and swaying gently together. The scene fades to black and from the darkness we hear Karin's voice asking, "Why are you here?"

Matt's voice answers, and as he speaks, a series of images of Matt in a kind of video montage plays on the screen.

"I first came out here to the protest to bring my grand-mother cookies to remind her of home. I like to bake." The film shows Matt leaping over a log, chasing another boy.

"I thought it would be like a fun camp-out—like Scouts, you know?"

In this shot, Karin has caught Matt's face at sunset. His skin glows with the warm colours of that time of day, his mop of messy hair tumbles over his forehead. He squints a little as if he is studying something in the distance. Then, he must have heard Karin because he turns and looks directly at the camera and he grins with a cheeky sort of embarrassment and puts his hand up to hide his face.

Meanwhile, his voice continues to explain why he's in the forest. "But at night they don't tell ghost stories—they talk about the forest and stuff and about the difference between the old-growth forests and the second-growth trees and how important it is to preserve the diverse species that live in the ancient forests."

Now there's a picture of a huge old cedar tree. At first, it isn't obvious that Matt is anywhere in the picture, but as Karin zooms in to show the foot of the tree up close you can see Matt sitting on the ground with his back up against the massive trunk. He's so small and he's wearing a brown sweater and pants so he blends in like one of those forest creatures that relies on camouflage for survival.

"Trees aren't just trees, you know. If they cut these trees down, they won't grow back by the time I'm grown up or even by the time my grandchildren grow up. So now I think I have to try to do something to make people see that these trees aren't just any ordinary trees. Do you know what I mean?"

Here, a close-up image of Matt's lips matches the words he's speaking. Karin has edited this piece of film so it repeats, "Do you know what I mean? Do you know what I mean? Do you know what I mean?"

Then another voice fades in saying, "What I mean is, I'm glad someone is finally paying attention."

I recognize the voice right away, even before the screen shows a close-up of the old woman's hand crooked around a burning cigarette.

"I was born in a cabin in the forest right over there."

The camera follows the arc of the woman's gesture and pans over the barren landscape of the clear-cut.

I steal a glance at Karin. She notices and flashes me a quick grin.

Then, Matt's voice echoes again, "Do you know what I mean?"

When the screen goes all fuzzy I'm so jealous that Karin can say with a minute of film what I can't seem to say in hundreds of words. I guess maybe it's because she can have her characters speak for themselves but as a writer I have to filter everything through my brain and hands.

"Cool," Eric says.

It is cool. But for some reason nobody wants to say anything else.

Gillian sits motionless, staring at the notebook in her lap. I wonder if she's still going to send in her letter to the editor. Surely she can see now that Matt isn't just being bullied into staying with the protesters. He may be young, but he's smart, way smarter than people would think. The silence stretches until everyone shifts uncomfortably.

When Custer says, "Does anyone want to see my new *Space Ratz Adventure*?" I want to hug him. "I brought enough copies so everyone can look at the pictures."

"Perfect!" I say, and jump up to grab the pile of carefully assembled mini comic books he has pulled out of his folder. As I'm handing them out to the others, I study the drawing on the cover, which shows a distorted rat wearing a bubble-shaped space helmet. Thank goodness there are no trees in space!

Though the unpleasant tension doesn't completely go away, we manage to find plenty to say about the comic strip. When we're done, Karin says, "Hey guys. You've had time to think. I really want some feedback."

"I love watching movies," Eric says. We all nod. Who doesn't?

"That's not the point," Karin says. "How can I make my documentary better if you don't tell me what you like—or don't like."

"Yeah," Willow drawls. "It's not like every movie is, like, brilliant just because it's a movie."

"Obviously," I say. But for some reason it's harder to come up with good suggestions for Karin than it is to criticize something on paper.

"I like the close-ups of Matt," Wynd ventures, and this finally gets the ball rolling. Throughout the whole discussion, Gillian stays silent and never looks at me, quite an accomplishment given the size of the room.

As usual, Eric wants more drama and wonders why Karin didn't shoot anything showing Matt getting arrested. Both Wynd and Willow are impressed with the clear-cut.

"Was that old woman a protester?" Wynd asks.

"No," Willow says, punching her lightly in the shoulder. Then she pauses. "She isn't, is she?"

Karin scribbles something in her notebook. "No. She lives near there. But that's obviously not clear enough. I'll have to fix that."

Then Custer asks, "Don't people change when you film them?"

"What do you mean?"

"You're trying to show people in real life, right? Like, how they really are?"

"Yeah. So?"

I know what he means. "When you pointed the camera at me, I got really irritated. So you couldn't really get shots of anyone being themselves—not really. When the camera's there, people change."

Karin keeps scribbling. Eric seems determined to keep the meeting as normal as possible. "Have you heard enough?" he asks Karin.

"Thanks," she says, still writing. "That's great."

"How about we finish up with an easy writing exercise?" he asks, sounding more like forty than fourteen.

"What do we have to do?" Karin asks.

"Use these words in a poem." Eric reads from a sheet of paper, "Sheet, jam, elbow, picture, country, cookie," and then flips the page onto the coffee table. "Five minutes. Go."

For five blissful minutes there is no sound but the furious scribbling of pens. There's no time to think of anything but putting one word after another.

We read our efforts aloud and then Willow suggests the homework assignment. "We have to write a scene set in a café. Two people meet for coffee and one of them has a secret."

"Do you have to tell the secret?" Custer asks.

Willow shrugs. "Doesn't matter."

Gillian has already packed up her stuff and zips out the door before I've even closed my notebook. I tug my scarf around my neck, organize my books in my arms, and turn to push out the door. Before I can get my weight behind my shoulder to give the door a good shove, it swings open and I topple forward. I would have wiped out completely if Custer's father hadn't extended a hand to steady me.

"Sorry about that," he says with a chuckle. "You're Heather, right?"

Something tells me I should lie but my head nods despite my reservations.

"I thought so." He extends his hand and then pulls it back when he realizes that there's no way I can juggle my stuff for a handshake.

"Alexander Ryerson. I'm an accountant with Burton International."

Twin desires—one to bolt past Mr. Ryerson and the other to tell him my name is really Gillian and I'm a little confused—scramble in my head. Fortunately, or unfortunately, depending on how I choose to look at this development, Mr. Ryerson seems to have plenty to say.

"I've been following your articles in the paper. Very interesting. You are quite a talented writer."

He doesn't even give me time to say thank you for the compliment, but I'm not all that convinced he really means it as a compliment anyway.

"However"—oh, great, here it comes—"it seems as though it might be hard for you to speak to anyone objective within the industry." He smiles at me and slips a business card into my notebook. "If you ever need an insider to interview, why don't you give me a call?"

"Hi, Dad!" Custer says from behind me.

"Hey, kiddo. Ready to go?"

"Yeah. Can we stop at the video store on the way home?"

Mr. Ryerson checks his watch. "We're a little late tonight. How about we go tomorrow after school?"

I don't hear Custer's answer because father and son sweep out through the door and disappear into the dark.

"He seems like a pretty nice guy," Karin says from right behind me. I spin around to face her.

"I didn't know you were there."

"Eric and I were just making sure everything was turned off." She nods toward the door. "It's hard to hate someone like that, isn't it?"

"I don't want to hate anybody," I say. "I really don't."

Karin shifts the weight of her shoulder bag and shakes

her head. "Nobody wants to hate, I don't think. But nobody wants to be wrong, either. That just sucks."

"That's almost profound," I say, and we both laugh.

The door swings open again and one of Karin's moms walks in, the short one who likes flowing scarves, the one Karin calls Bee. "Oh good, you're done. Hi, Heather."

"Hi."

"Did you have a good meeting?"

I nod, too exhausted to even think about that simple question too carefully.

"Have you got everything, sweetie?" she says to Karin and then turns back to me. "I think your dad is out there in the parking lot."

"Thanks. Goodnight, Eric," I call back into the community centre as the last light turns off.

"See you next week!" he says as he catches up to me on the front steps. The door bangs behind us and we head to our respective cars and parents and lives. If I had superpowers, I would use them right about now to perform a magical switch and disappear into the plush leather seats of Eric's car and drive off into the night with his glamorous, jazz-singing mother who probably has no idea that there are trees on this island that people are willing to risk everything for.

25

Never bend your head. Always hold it high. Look the world straight in the face. – Helen Keller

Saturday February 26th

There is a saying, "Be careful what you wish for because you just might get it." Now I think I know what that means because when Granny asked me if I wanted to go to Victoria on a shopping trip I secretly wished that I wouldn't have to go. Granny will be in court next week and her lawyer thinks there is a good chance that she will still be in jail for all of spring break. The problem is that it takes time to organize a trial and Granny says that she has every right in a free country to protest against something she doesn't believe is good for society and the environmental health of the planet. This means she won't sign the forms they want her to sign to promise she won't go back to the logging road and that means they won't let her out of jail because she is likely to be a repeat offender.

Words. Labels. Repeat offender. Like she's a drug addict or habitual bank robber or something. Even though sometimes she makes me so mad. I can't see her like that, not really. She is still just Granny and I guess I really do want to go shopping with her. Except now we can't. At least not during this spring break.

That's it for now. I smell pancakes!

The phone rings just as Matt is tipping three perfect miniature pancakes onto my plate. Dad grabs the phone with one hand while he continues to pour coffee into his mug with the other. "Hello?"

I smear a healthy dollop of butter on my pancakes and am just reaching for the syrup when Dad laughs and says, "Well! For goodness' sake. I hardly recognize your voice! How are you doing? And how are your mom and dad? Good. Ah-ha. Well, say hello from all of us. I suppose you'd like to talk to Heather?"

"Who is it?" I mouth, but Dad just grins and hands me the phone. Then he nudges Matt, who is so distracted that he hasn't flipped the current batch of pancakes bubbling on the griddle.

"Hello?"

"Hey theeeeeere."

"Mags!" Dad shoos me away and I stretch the phone cord through the door and out into the hall.

"How come you haven't written to me? I was waiting for you to send me a list of the stuff you sent, you know— the psychic images."

"Well, you didn't exactly send me anything and I did try to call, but you weren't there, so I thought maybe you didn't even remember to do it, and then I kind of got busy."

"I bet. Your grandmother is sure in a lot of trouble."

"Who told you?" I rack my brains trying to think who would even know that Mags knows Granny. Matt?

"Wouldn't you like to know!"

"Tell me!"

On the other end of the line Mags giggles. She knows she has me. I gasp. "You don't mean that's what you received in our psychic experiment. Because that's not what I sent!"

Now Mags is laughing pretty hard. "You're just as gullible as ever!" she says. "Don't you know what a big story this is? Your grandmother and some of those other naked ladies were on the news here. They weren't naked on the news, but the interviewer did hold up a picture of Mrs. October from that calendar. My mom wants a copy."

I shake my head. Unbelievable. Ontario is thousands of kilometres away. Why do they care about this stuff? They cut all their trees down hundreds of years ago.

"I think it's pretty cool what they're doing. I can't believe your grandmother went to jail. That seems kind of harsh. Nothing exciting like that ever happens here."

Bizarre as it seems, Mags actually sounds jealous.

"It's not boring, that's for sure."

"So," Mags says. "What did you send for a picture?"

"Oh, no," I say. "Tell me what you think you received and then I'll tell you what I sent. Otherwise you might be unduly influenced by the power of suggestion."

"Only you would say something like that!" Mags laughs again and I just want her to keep on joking and laughing forever. I never want to hang up the phone. I want to crawl right through the wire all the way to Toronto and curl up with Mags and a bowl of popcorn to watch a goofy movie. "You haven't changed at all," she adds, though she isn't laughing any more. "Fine. I'll tell you what I saw. I saw a woodbox and a rabbit."

I have to think for a moment to see if there is any way that either the starfish or the card could have been misinterpreted.

"Hmm. Not quite. I had that card you made me once, the friendship one with the two girls with the red hair ribbons on it? Remember?"

"Um . . . kind of. Didn't you make me one, too?"

"You mean you don't have it on your bedside table so it's the last thing you see at night?"

"Ummm . . . oh, yeah . . . that's right."

"Never mind. The second thing was this really cool starfish."

"Starfish? Are you sure?"

"Positive."

"No rabbit?"

"Nope."

She sighs. "Oh well. Clearly we need to practise more. What about you? What did you receive?"

"Dumb stuff. I'm sure you didn't send any of it. Hang on a second while I go and get the list."

I race upstairs, retrieve the list, and am back on the phone in seconds. "Are you there? Okay. Ponytail. Hair clips. Hairbrush. Footstool. Carpet. Worms. Mr. Saunderson. Sleigh bells."

By this point in the list, Mags is having hysterics. She can hardly breathe.

"I'm not finished."

"Sorry," she gasps. "Keep going. I'll be quiet."

"Bride. Slippery. Tow truck. Chocolate coins wrapped in gold foil. Candy necklace. Jam—I can still hear you!"

"How can you hear me? I covered the mouthpiece."

"I'm not going to read the rest. It's too stupid. Have I got anything right?"

"No. Not really."

"Maybe it would be quicker if you told me what you were sending and I'll tell you if it's on my list."

"Just read. This is very entertaining. Your mind is a pretty fascinating junk pile."

"Fleas. Canoe race. Red-beard pirate. Those fish that eat people."

"Piranhas?"

"Yeah, that's it. I couldn't spell it."

"Psychics don't have to spell."

"Then I drew a picture of a teepee and some arrows that kind of point to the word *locked* and then I drew a circle around the word *ambulance*. And that's it."

I feel completely and utterly foolish. What a waste of a good long-distance phone conversation. "So, what did you think about?"

"Well, I was lying on my bed looking at the ceiling and you know how there's that water stain right above my bed that looks like a big monster spider?"

"Not really."

"Well, there is. Oh, maybe the bathroom flooded after

you left. Anyway, I was trying to concentrate on that except I was so hungry I couldn't stand it. My stomach kept growling and Mom was downstairs baking cinnamon buns."

"What?"

"Cinnamon buns. What, don't they have cinnamon buns out in B.C.?"

"Of course they do. But I stopped receiving because I kept smelling baking! And it was cinnamon that I smelled—but Matt wasn't making cinnamon buns, he was making banana muffins! I didn't think anything of it at the time."

We are both silent for a long moment.

"Wow," Mags says at last. "That's pretty cool."

"Do you think that means something? Do you think—"

"For sure," she says. "How else could you explain it?"

All the hairs along my arms stand straight up and I shiver as if someone has opened the door and let in an icy draft.

"I don't want to do it again," she says.

"Me neither," I agree.

We chat for a little longer until her mother calls her away from the phone. We promise to call more often and to kick our family members off our computers so we can send email. Then I head back into the kitchen to finish breakfast, very glad that Matt has made pancakes and not cinnamon buns.

26

One has to live a life that creates a writer.

— Erno Paasilinna

Renegade Grandmother Is Both Right and Wrong

By Heather Blake

What my grandmother has done may be against the law, but it is not a criminal act. And that says to me that maybe somebody should be looking at the law. I'm just a kid, so I can't do that. But if it seems like a good idea to me then I can at least write about it so maybe a lawyer or a judge or whoever actually makes laws can try to change things. Maybe someone can figure out how to make things work in a better way so people can safely protest the things they don't like and other people don't have to worry about losing a lot of income.

Canada is a good country and I'm glad that I live here. But now I know it isn't perfect. I also know that smart people are thinking about how to make things better and this makes me feel more optimistic about the future. But I also know that I can't just let other people look after everything for me and that's why I'm writing this article even though it will probably make somebody else mad at me.

The role of writers is not to change the way the legal system deals with protesters. It's more like we have to shine a light in the dark corners of our society so others might have a chance to see a way out.

What I've learned during the past weeks is that when people are mad they don't always make the best decisions but that sometimes we have to get mad about something before we can think about it properly. I know that has been true for me.

I still wouldn't choose to do some of the things my grandmother has done in order to draw attention to something I find upsetting (like just because I find the fact that 24 percent of Canadians are considered to be illiterate doesn't mean I would ever make a nude calendar), but I'm not mad at her any more. Instead, I'm trying to understand why someone who has a very nice life and family, someone who is gentle and normal in every way, would get so upset that she would do something so many people don't like. And by listening to what she and the other Ladies of the Forest have to say, I have learned that they do have a point about those old trees.

But I have also listened to the children whose dads work in the woods and to a person who works in the forestry company office and to people who have businesses on this island and to the police officer who detained my little brother and by listening to them all I know that there is no simple answer to the trouble in our Tarragon Woods and, more than that, the trouble in our legal system. But I do believe there is an answer if enough people sit down and talk for long enough. While it's obvious that there's not much point in talking if somebody rushes in and chops down all those trees, we can't get the talking started if we stay at home and hide.

And this is why I will be going back to school next week. One way or the other, I have work to do, and I can only do it out there in the ugliness of the real world.

Gillian's letter is also in the paper. I don't have to love it, but I guess I'm glad they printed it. I feel very generous thinking this, though I can't actually bring myself to read the whole thing.

The second thing in this week's paper that is written by me is much shorter than my opinion piece but just as important. It's a little notice about our literacy project, letting people know where they can drop off their gently used books so we can start collecting materials for our tutoring program. Everyone in the group has been busy phoning anyone who might be able to help. Eric called the community centre for me and they have agreed to let us start a special library there just for the program.

It's actually getting pretty exciting and I'm already looking forward to our first reading sessions after spring break. Eric is thinking of helping out and Karin wants to come to our next Kids Helping Kids meeting to get some footage about how kids can organize community projects without very much help from adults. She said it would make a good companion film to the one she is making about old people who decide to become protest-ers. I figure that if she comes she might be able to get us some good publicity.

I think that maybe she is grateful that when the time came to vote on whether or not she could stay in the writing group I voted to let her stay. Only Wynd said no, but she did the same thing to Custer. I noticed that she put her hand up after she had seen that all the rest of us were voting yes, so she knew it wouldn't make a difference. Sometimes Wynd just needs to be seen to be doing things her own way. Whatever. This is a democ-racy. Everyone has a right to an opinion.

27

Great is the art of beginning, but greater is the art of ending. – Henry Wadsworth Longfellow

"Heather! Good to see you back!"

Mrs. Gurney stands and reaches across her desk to take my hand. Her grip is firm and certain, not at all what I would have expected. I thought for sure she would have one of those limp-fish kind of handshakes that Mom absolutely despises. I remember when Matt and I were really little we had handshake lessons from Mom and that's where I learned to look someone in the eye and give a nice, solid squeeze when shaking hands. I do just that with Mrs. Gurney and then she gestures at the chair in front of her desk.

"I'm not sure that I can guarantee—"

I hold my hand up and interrupt. "This isn't about my locker or anything."

"Oh? Then why . . . "

She tilts her head to one side and I feel a wee squeal of triumph in my belly that I really am the one in control of this meeting. It makes me feel ridiculously happy.

"You know that I am involved with the Kids Helping Kids group?"

A look of vague concern crosses her face. I suppose she thinks maybe I'm going to set up a protest or something outside the school. I decide not to let her suffer for too long and pull out several posters from my bag.

"Did you know that a significant number of people in this country do not know how to read well enough to fill out a job application form?"

She smiles, clearly relieved, and says, "As a matter of fact, I have heard something about that."

I smile back at her, thoroughly enjoying myself now. "Well, we have decided to raise money for schools in poor countries to buy books. We're also collecting books to use for tutoring younger kids here on the island who are having trouble reading."

Mrs. Gurney pulls one of the posters that Matt made across the desk toward her and pulls her reading glasses up onto her nose from where they hang on a chain around her neck. "Oh, I see—this is a good idea. Would you like a few minutes in assembly to make an announcement?"

"That would be great. Thank you. We have another program, too."

"You've certainly been busy during your time off!"

"You could say! We're looking for teenagers to volunteer to help the kids with their reading. And I've got a collection box that I could maybe put out in the front hall where people could drop off their gently used books."

Mrs. Gurney is remarkably cooperative. I suppose she is so relieved that we aren't talking about vandalism or arson or attacks on my person that she is willing to help with the literacy stuff in any way she can.

"I'd better get going to class," I say, finally.

"Yes. Yes, certainly. Off you go."

I get up to leave and as I reach the door she says, "Heather?" When I stop and turn back to her she stands and offers me her hand again. This time the handshake is slower, more thoughtful, though just as firm. "Good for you," she says, and then lets me go.

Posters in hand, I head for the bulletin board across from the office. The halls are crowded with kids arriving for school. The noise, as usual, is deafening. Jerry Bastion shoves one of his cap kid friends and he, in turn, bumps into me. We turn, and for just a moment he doesn't look away and neither do I.

And then I smile at him. Not a big, goofy, soppy smile or anything. It's just a small "I know you didn't mean to do that" smile, but it's enough that he gives me a wink, so quick that none of his friends notice, and then he swaggers away from me, punching Jerry in the shoulder and letting out an ear-splitting whoop.

I turn back to the wall and move aside a notice about basketball tryouts so there's room right in the middle of the board for our poster. I figure the reading project is far more important. I mean, this is the kind of thing that could change the world.

Anchoring it firmly at all four corners with pins that Alyssum made me bring along, I pause a moment to make sure that the phone number is correct. Then I check my watch and jog off down the hall to math class.

Once again I ignore the subject at hand and pull out my notebook and balance it on my lap under my desk.

Dear Granny,

I have never written to a prisoner before! Do the guards read your mail? I feel like a criminal myself—I'm writing to you instead of doing math.

It doesn't seem like it would be very nice to remind you of what life is like out here, though Dad said you would probably enjoy reading about normal things. Even math?

I'm putting a copy of my two new articles in with this letter, but you'll see that there's another clipping, too—the one about the meeting notice.

There's this guy, a writer from the Kootenays, who is coming to Tarragon Island to run a meeting about maybe starting a community forest project in the Tarragon Woods. He started something like that where he lives and I guess some people think it's a pretty good idea.

I don't know exactly what he's thinking (the meeting hasn't happened yet), but I thought I would go with Matt, Uma, and Alyssum to show that young people are interested in these kinds of things.

I wanted to tell you something else, too, something that I kind of need to say in case they never let you out of jail (kidding!). I like the idea of a meeting, of figuring out a better way to do things. But this meeting wouldn't have happened if the protesters hadn't clogged up the road, if they weren't still out there. And it probably wouldn't have happened if you and your friends hadn't made that calendar. The trees would be long gone by now and nobody as far away as the Kootenays would even have heard about what was going on.

As it is, did you know that they have opened an account at the credit union to accept donations for things like your lawyer? (Mom is happy about that!) But they are also saying they can use the money to do a study, or build a mill, or furniture-making school, or whatever. (Actually, I don't think anyone else has mentioned the furniture-making school—I'm thinking it might be a good idea, though.)

So I guess maybe when things have to change (did you ever go up and look at that clear-cut? You must have, I guess), there are different ways to help.

Mom says we can go with Dad to the trial. It looks like it will happen in spring break. Did you think that's how we'd spend our day in Victoria? Me neither.

I'll be sitting as close to the front as I can and I'll be wearing that fuchsia skirt we bought the last time we went shopping together—you know, the one with the swirl of tiny white flowers? I haven't worn that one for a while— but you helped me pick it out, remember? It makes my legs look longer.

Love, Heather

P. S. I just thought of something else. If you want to send me a letter about what you think about the community forest idea, I could take it to the meeting for you and read it on your behalf. Just understand that I will stay fully dressed from start to finish!

Other books by Nikki Tate
Available from Sono Nis Press

The StableMates Series
StableMates 1: Rebel of Dark Creek
StableMates 2: Team Trouble at Dark Creek
StableMates 3: Jessa Be Nimble, Rebel Be Quick
StableMates 4: Sienna's Rescue
StableMates 5: Raven's Revenge
StableMates 6: Return to Skoki Lake
StableMates 7: Keeping Secrets at Dark Creek

The Tarragon Island Series
Tarragon Island
No Cafés in Narnia

The Estorian Chronicles
Book One: Cave of Departure
Book Two: Battle for Carnillo

Author's Note

A little more than half of the world's temperate rainforests have already been destroyed. Approximately one quarter of the remaining temperate rainforests are located in British Columbia. This figure represents approximately half of the old-growth forests we started with—the rest have already been cut. These ancient forests and the complex ecosystems they support also happen to contain some of the world's most valuable wood. Where there is money to be made, there is tremendous pressure to harvest that wood. The cheapest and easiest methods of harvesting the trees are usually not the methods that preserve the environment for future generations.

Organizations like the Women in the Woods (a direct-action environmental group based in British Columbia) believe that protecting what is left of the public forests is essential to the survival of our planet and humankind. The fact that peaceful protests may send these women to jail (most, though not all, of the group members are women) does not lessen their determination. Many have been arrested, some more than once, but they see direct action as one of the few methods the average citizen can use to participate in the democratic process and actually have an effect on government policy. The passion of these women for their cause cannot be denied. One group member in her late seventies wrote, "If we indiscriminately cut away our 'old-growth trees' we are also indiscriminately cut[ting] away parts of ourselves." Similarly, founding member Betty Krawczyk, herself a great-grandmother, says, "These ancient forests hold the history of human and animal evolution as well as the earth's evolution. We humans evolved with these awesome wonders, and to degrade them for the momentary profit of a few is to degrade the human race and the earth itself."

One battle between logging companies and citizens wanting to protect an old-growth forest took place in Clayoquot Sound on the west coast of Vancouver Island. In 1993 the Clayoquot Peace Camp became the home base for the largest blockade in Canadian history. The protest at Clayoquot was the largest act of peaceful civil disobedience in this country and resulted in more than 850 arrests. As one group was taken away, new protesters arrived to take their place. Men, women, and children who took part in the blockade were removed and many of these protesters spent time in jail because, according to the courts, they were breaking the law.

This incident (a number of people I knew were arrested; many more took place in the protests) and subsequent direct-action environmental protests forced me to think hard about the role of the individual in the democratic process. Is it ever acceptable to break the law if you feel strongly that the law is wrong? Do peaceful protesters have a role to play in changing government policy? What is the price an individual pays when he or she decides to take on the law?

The fact that many environmental activists are women and many of these women are grandmothers made me question what role older members of our society should play in shaping the policies and laws affecting all citizens. Just because someone is old, is he or she necessarily wise?

The more people I spoke to, the better I came to know those willing to risk everything, even their own freedom, and the more I wanted to write about the difficult dilemmas faced by ordinary people involved in extraordinary circumstances.

Trouble on Tarragon Island was the result. My hope for this book is that it will encourage people to ask questions, to consider what is most important to them, and then decide how best to become involved in the complex decision-making process we call democracy.

Trouble on Tarragon Island is rooted in fact. Versions of the incidents described really happened here in our British Columbia communities. An angry truck driver really did try to run me over. Children at the Clayoquot Sound protests really were taken into custody by the RCMP. Loggers really do lose their jobs when parks are created. Women pose nude for calendars to bring attention to their cause. Activists receive death threats. Logging industry executives struggle to find financially viable solutions in a difficult industry. Laws are slow to change.

Yes, this is a work of fiction. But stories just like this are being told over and over again in communities around the world. It is up to each one of us to decide how we would like to shape these stories so they have the happiest endings possible. It doesn't matter whether your passion is creating a new bike trail, encouraging spay-neuter programs to reduce the number of unwanted pets, cleaning up a local salmon-bearing stream or neighbourhood park, or saving a single old cedar tree. Learn all you can about the issue and find a way to get involved. Who knows, maybe one day someone will write a book about what you have accomplished!

About the Author

Born in England, Nikki Tate travelled the world before settling down on a tiny farm on Vancouver Island. Horses, goats, birds, cats, dogs, and koi keep her busy when she isn't dreaming up ideas for new books. Active as a literacy advocate, Tate chairs the Victoria Children's Literature Roundtable and the Vancouver Island Council of the International Reading Association, regularly reviews children's books, and speaks to parents and educators about reading, writing, and literacy, at venues all over North America. Tate also works as a professional storyteller, retelling the stories of King Arthur's court. She is a popular writing workshop leader for both adults and children.